# Alone in a New World
## The New World Book Three

Sherry Derr-Wille

ISBN: 978-1-62420-606-1

Credits
Cover Artist: Designs by Ms G
Editor: Amanda Armstrong

# Dedication

To all of my family, friends and fans who have been waiting for this series to materialize.

# Chapter One
## October, 2104

Jason Culver was on the late-night patrol in Elko, Nevada. He checked the communicator on his wrist and saw the time was four thirty in the morning. His shift would be ending in two and a half hours. This was going to be his last late shift. Beginning Monday, he would be transferring to the day shift of the Elko Police Department. He was more than ready to get on a regular day schedule like most of the other people in the world. What he did realize was this had been a good shift for him, at least when he was single. Most people were at home in bed and not out making mischief or breaking laws. On the day shift he would see much more action.

His mental musings were interrupted when he saw something in the under lights of his hovercraft that caused him to land and go to investigate what seemed to be too bizarre to be true.

As soon as he landed, he left his craft and hurried to where a little boy, wearing pajamas with no shoes, stood on the sidewalk crying.

"I'm Officer Culver," he said as he approached the child. "Where is your mother?"

The boy sniffed loudly and proclaimed in heavily accented English, "My mama won't wake up."

Jason knelt in front of the child. "What's your name?"

"Marco."

"Do you know where you live?"

He nodded his head and pointed to an apartment complex.

"Did you have a bad dream?"

Marco shook his head.

"It's very late. This is the time when everyone should be in bed sleeping. Let me take you to your apartment. I'm certain your mother is very worried about you."

Again, Marco shook his head. "She's been asleep for a long time.

I tried to wake her up when I got up in the daytime. She wouldn't wake up. I'm hungry."

Jason noticed the child's words, although they were spoken in English, sometimes sounded more like Spanish. Looking closer, he could tell the boy was of Mexican descent. It was possible his mother was in the country illegally. There could be drugs involved. Anything was possible.

Picking Marco up, he made his way inside the building. After checking the listing of tenants, he saw the name Tessa Almanor. It was the only name that sounded as though it could be Mexican. The apartment number beside the name was two fifty-two.

Rather than taking the elevator, Jason carried Marco up the stairs to the second floor. The door with the right number stood open. Before entering, Jason put the child down.

"I'm going to check on your mother. You stay here."

His heart pounded almost out of his chest as he made his way through the dark apartment. He shone his flashlight around the neat living room as well as the pristine kitchen. It looked like Tessa kept a clean house. To his right was a hallway. It led down to a bathroom and two doors that looked like they led into bedrooms. In the first room, he saw a single bed, with decorations that denoted it belonged to a small child. Moving on, he went into the other room where he could see a woman sleeping on the bed.

"Ms. Almanor? Can you hear me?"

When he received no response, he touched her shoulder. To his horror, her skin was cold and her body stiff. It was evident she'd been dead for several hours.

He immediately contacted his superior officer on his communicator. He also requested the medical examiner as well as social services and backup.

Remembering Marco, he hurried back out into the hall. The child was still whimpering, although now his cries weren't loud, big tears rolled down his cheeks as he sucked his thumb.

"Do you know where your father is?" Jason asked.

Without taking his thumb from his mouth, Marco shook his head no.

"Do you have other family here in town?"

Again, the child indicated no.

It wasn't long before social services arrived and took the child away. With his duty to little Marco finished, he returned to the apartment. He started going through the rooms, looking for any information that would help him find the family of either the deceased woman or the child. He was shocked to see there were no papers identifying either Tessa or Marco. It was entirely possible those weren't even their names.

"What do we have here?" his superior officer asked when he entered the apartment with the medical examiner.

"I saw a little boy out on the sidewalk at four thirty this morning. He was wearing pajamas with no shoes and he was crying. He said his mother wouldn't wake up. I was certain he'd had a bad dream and woke up frightened. I brought him into this building and surmised the apartment rented under the name of Tessa Almanor had to belong to his mother. I left him in the hall and found his mother in the bedroom. It's evident she's been dead for several hours."

"Do you suspect foul play?"

Jason thought for a moment "I don't think so. The apartment is too neat to have a murder take place here, there are no signs of a struggle. There also wasn't any blood that I could see. It's possible she died of natural causes."

"Where is the boy now?"

"Social services got here before you did. They took him. He was very distraught and he said he was hungry. He's only three, maybe four, and just thinks his mother is sleeping. From what I gathered, he tried to wake her up yesterday when he got up and he couldn't. He's probably been alone ever since. It's possible he went out onto the street to see if someone could wake up his mother."

"Well, if that don't beat all. We've got to find out where the kid's father or any other relatives are. If we don't…"

Before his supervisor could continue, the medical examiner came out of the bedroom. "I won't know anything until we do an autopsy, but it looks like she might have suffered either a massive heart attack or an aneurism. What have you found out about her identity?"

"Next to nothing," Jason replied. "We'll know more when we can talk to the owner of this apartment building in the morning. He can probably shed some light on her background."

~ * ~

The woman who took Marco's hand and led him away from the apartment he'd shared with his mother seemed nice enough. She tried to ask him several questions, but he remembered what his mother told him about talking to strangers.

*We can't let him find us, Marco. If he does, he'll take you away from me and I'll never see you again.*

His mother's words of warning rang in his head. Remembering them, he could hear the bad man who wanted Marco to call him Papa. They ran away from him and left their home in Arizona in the middle of the night. He also remembered his mother calling him Paco but telling him from now on he would be called Marco.

Even though the nice lady got him some food to eat, he knew he had to protect the secret his mother told him never to tell.

~ * ~

Two weeks into the investigation, Jason knew no more about Tessa Almanor than he had the morning he found her dead in her bed.

He didn't know how many times he'd read the report from the medical examiner. What it showed was that in the past she'd suffered a severe beating, so severe that it caused her a slow and painful death from the internal bruising. It was entirely possible she'd been slowly bleeding internally for several days, if not weeks.

The interview with the owner of the apartment building didn't give them any more information than they already had. Tessa and her son moved into the furnished apartment less than two weeks before her death and she'd paid him cash for the first two month's rent. Other than that, he had no further information. Knowing the area where the apartment building was located, he realized cash talked very loudly and often it paid for no questions asked about someone's past.

To add insult to injury, he'd heard from social services that since no family could be found for Marco, he'd been sent to a boy's ranch in a remote area of Nevada called Henderson Ranch. It was probably the best thing that could have happened to the boy. He would be able to grow up in a healthy environment. Being an orphan, as well as his Mexican heritage, made his chances of being adopted slim to none.

# Chapter Two

Marco didn't want to believe his mother was dead, but that was what the lady at the social services office told him. He didn't think she would lie to him, but he still wanted his mother to come and get him. The bad man didn't know where they were, and they had a nice place to live.

He stayed at the social service house for a week, before a man by the name of Mr. Henderson came to take him away.

"You'll be living on our ranch now," Mr. Henderson said as he packed Marco's meager belongings into his hovercraft. "You'll like it there. We have horses you can ride and other children for you to play with."

Marco was hopeful, but everything changed when they arrived at the remote ranch. He was taken to a building where the walls were lined with beds. He saw a few small children but not enough to fill all of the beds.

"Do you speak Spanish?" Mr. Henderson asked, as he led Marco to the lower bunk that would become his.

"Si," he replied, hoping to impress the man with his knowledge of both languages. "My mama and I speak both English and Spanish."

Mr. Henderson smiled and nodded. "We'll help you to recall all of your Spanish and to talk English better too. It will be helpful when you grow up."

Once the man left the building, Marco sat on his bed. He was frightened, but he decided it was best if he didn't tell anyone much about either his mother or the bad man they'd run away from when he was called Paco.

He must have fallen asleep, because he was startled awake by the voices of boys entering the room.

"You're new here," a boy with very dark hair and piercing brown eyes said. "My name is Christopher, what's your name?"

Marco looked at the boy and decided he wasn't much older than himself. Being careful to perpetuate the lie he and his mother had been living, he answered, "I'm Marco."

"This is Peter. He doesn't talk much until he gets to know you. I sleep over here and Peter sleeps over there." He pointed to the bunk bed on the opposite side of the room after indicating the bunk next to Marco's as being his.

"I bet you ain't got no folks, just like us," Peter said.

"My mama died. At least that's what they told me."

Peter nodded. "My ma was a dirty whore, that's what Mr. Henderson said. She went to prison and nobody else wanted me. You got a pa?"

Marco shook his head no. The bad man wanted Marco to call him Papa but Mama said he shouldn't call him that.

"Christopher ain't got no folks either. They told him that his pa was killed in a hovercraft crash and his ma died after he was born. Don't know if that's true, but it's a good story. Henderson told us to come in and get you for supper. If you don't eat now, you don't get nothin' until morning."

Thinking about eating a meal brought back memories of the delicious meals his mother served. His mouth watered thinking about having meat, potatoes and vegetables, with the seasonings his mother used to make them taste good. It wasn't that the people at social services didn't give him good food but it wasn't the same as the things his mama made for him.

While Peter and Christopher ate their food with great gusto, Marco was sadly disappointed. He could find no meat or vegetables in the watery soup and the other unidentifiable food that was put on his plate had no taste.

"When do we get our meat?" Marco whispered to Christopher.

"We only get meat once a week. This is what we get and we have to like it. It ain't so bad once you get used to it."

*I'll never get used to this. I want my mama. I want to eat the food she used to make for me.*

Having been told this was all he was going to get to eat, he gagged down the food. It was either that or starve. Knowing that, he decided he wanted to live and make his mama proud of him.

~ * ~

As the months went on, Marco, Peter and Christopher became fast friends. He also noticed that one by one, the older boys no longer played with them. He soon learned that as soon as the boys reached the age of six, they went out to work the ranch with the other older boys. From what he could tell it was hard work, but Mr. Henderson said it was how the older boys earned their keep and it was the duty of all the older kids to help out on the ranch.

By the time Marco neared the age of six he was used to eating only two meals a day. Games of tag, as well as hide and go seek, gave way to training, with lessons of roping along with learning to ride horses.

To Marco's disappointment, both Peter and Cristopher went out to work with the ranch hands, leaving Marco to become the instructor for the younger kids who were now learning the skills he'd mastered over the years.

It was a bright fall morning when Mr. Henderson came into the dormitory and told Marco that today was his birthday and from here on in, he would be working on the ranch, like the rest of his friends.

He soon learned the meager morning meal that was meant to sustain him all day left him starving by the time the sun was high in the sky. Spending hours in the saddle, herding cattle, was more exhausting than the lessons he'd engaged in over the previous months.

After the first week, he complained that he was hungry and tired. His reward for his complaints was being sent into the house where Mrs. Henderson made him pull down his pants so she could paddle him with the board that brought tears to his eyes.

When Mr. Henderson saw the tears staining his cheeks, he took him out to the box. It was the first time he'd been made aware of this punishment and he decided he never wanted to spend time there again. He could do nothing other than sit there for the allotted time, no matter how much his butt hurt from the paddling he'd received at the hands of Mrs. Henderson.

~ * ~

Years passed and Marco made the best of his situation. He soon learned he enjoyed working the ranch. It was the same with Peter, but he could tell Christopher hated every minute he spent in the saddle, taking care of the cattle.

"Have you noticed that Christopher isn't happy ranching?" Mr. Henderson asked one morning.

"I have," Marco replied.

"Well, you know the three of you will be turning eighteen soon. I know you and Peter will be able to get good jobs on ranches down in Mexico, but I worry about what Christopher will do. You might want to tell him about a group I heard about up in Idaho. They're young men like you and they might take Christopher in. He's white and so are they. You, on the other hand, wouldn't be accepted there. I want you to tell him about Patrick Ernst's group. He should be able to make his way up there without too much trouble."

Marco tended to agree with Mr. Henderson. Christopher was looking for something and it certainly wasn't ranching or carpentry.

It was about a week later when Christopher and Marco were rounding up the spring calves that Marco broached the subject of Patrick Ernst and the group of young men who served with him in the state of Idaho.

"You know," Marco began, "there's a group in Idaho where you might fit in. From what I heard it is a group of young men. Since you're white, they should take you in."

"What about you?" Christopher asked.

"I've got too much Mexican blood in me. Besides, Mr. Henderson tells me there are good jobs on the ranches down there. I can make good money and do what I know and love. I hope you will have as good a future with Patrick Ernst and his group as I will have on one of the ranches in Mexico."

Within two weeks, Christopher disappeared from Henderson Ranch. Marco missed his friend, but it made for a closer tie with Peter. The two of them talked about the future that looked so bright for both of them.

As ranch hands, they would have no need for a formal education. It didn't matter much to Marco. He knew what he needed to know to survive and make a living on a ranch.

Two months after Christopher left the ranch, it was Peter's turn. It was the same with him as it was with Christopher, it came without warning. One night, Peter was sleeping in the dormitory and the next morning, he was nowhere to be found.

Marco missed his two friends. They were the two best friends he could have asked for in life. He was certain their paths would not cross again, but he would never forget them.

~ * ~

October brought more changes to Marco's life. He was summoned to the main house where Mrs. Henderson gave him breakfast, before Mr. Henderson told him on this day he was now eighteen and it was time for him to go to Mexico and work on one of the ranches.

"I've contacted my friend, Carlos Gonzales, and he has a position for you doing the work you're so good at doing. I told him how good you are with the horses as well as the cattle and he's anxious to have you working with him."

Marco nodded. He'd been anticipating this. Soon he'd be free from the grueling work on Henderson Ranch and he would have a real job, working on a ranch in Mexico. He was also pleased that Mr. and Mrs. Henderson had insisted he speak Spanish with them whenever they were alone. He knew that Peter also spoke Spanish, but it wasn't the same with Christopher. He was never taught the language and spoke only English.

It seemed strange, but since Christopher wasn't as good at ranching as he and Peter were, it made sense. His life was going to take a different path and he probably wouldn't ever have a need to speak a second language.

Without so much as a goodbye to the other boys and young men who shared the dormitory, Marco climbed into the passenger seat of Mr. Henderson's hovercraft.

For the first time in fourteen years, Marco was leaving Henderson Ranch behind. His dreams of a life doing something he loved, being paid for his labor and taking pride in his future were about to come true.

After a three-hour flight, they landed on what looked like a prosperous ranch in southern Mexico. As soon as they docked the hovercraft, a middle-aged man approached them.

"Is this the one you were telling me about?" Carlos Gonzales asked.

"That's right, this is Marco. I think he's just what you need. He's good with both the cattle and the horses. He should be, I trained him myself."

The man approached Marco and roughly grabbed his hair. "Open your mouth, Slave," he ordered. "I want to see your teeth."

Horrified, Marco did as he was told.

"Now, take off those clothes. I ain't buying any damaged goods."

Unable to protest, he dropped his pants and took off his shirt. Once he stood, naked, Señor Gonzales grabbed his genitals.

"Hmm, he's well hung. There are times we make deals with other ranches who are breeding slaves. He might be a good breeder. In the meantime, he should work out well."

Once Marco was again dressed, he was horrified when Señor Gonzales put an electronic collar around his neck as well as one on his ankle.

"It's good to do business with you, Henderson. Can I ask, why you're bringing this one down? I mean what about Granger?"

"Things are getting tighter. You know, not as many bastards being brought to us by the state. I can't afford to split the profits with Granger."

"How much do you want for this one?"

"Since he's the best one I've sold you, I want double, fifty thousand dollars."

"From what I see, and what you tell me, he's worth it. It's less than I'd have to pay a top hand to work the ranch. The way I see it, I get free labor and you get paid for your time."

Marco looked from Gonzales to Henderson. "You old bastard," he spat. "How can you sell me as a slave?"

He no more than put voice to the question than an electric shock jolted his neck, forcing him to his knees.

"You'll learn your place, slave. From this day forward you belong to me. I've paid good money for you and you will do whatever I tell you to do. If I tell you to fuck another slave or let another one do it to you, there will be no backtalk. I have more ways to punish my slaves than just the electric shock. You'll learn I'm not someone to disobey."

Marco watched as Mr. Henderson got into his hovercraft and lifted off into the blue October sky.

# Chapter Three

If Marco thought life was hard on Henderson Ranch, it was paradise compared to the life he led as a slave working for Carlos Gonzales. He longed for the two meals that were served all the time he was growing up. As a slave he was given an evening meal of moldy bread, watery soup and rancid meat.

Days turned into weeks and weeks into months. Soon he'd been working as a slave for almost two years. During that time, he'd seen young men come and go. No one ever escaped, but many of them either died from malnutrition or were beaten to death for some infraction sometimes without proof.

Having grown up under the regime set up by the Hendersons, he knew better than to break the rules or not do as he was told.

For the past few days, he'd begun to realize his days of working on the ranch were coming to an end. More days than he could count, he had times when his vision blurred, and he had a hard time staying in the saddle. Death was only days away and for the first time he welcomed it.

In his dreams, he'd seen his mother, telling him how much she loved him and how sorry she was that she hadn't been able to raise him to adulthood.

Hanging onto the saddle horn, he rode into the dooryard of the Gonzales Ranch. For the past hour, he'd struggled to stay in the saddle, but managed to do so in order to avoid punishment. To his surprise, there was a strange hovercraft at the docking station.

"We're looking for Marco Almanor," he heard one of the men talking to Señor Gonzales say.

"I don't know who you're talking about."

With all the strength he could muster, Marco dismounted his horse. "I'm Marco," he said with the last of his energy.

After saying the words, the darkness he'd been fighting all day overtook him and he collapsed, knowing his life was at its end.

~ * ~

"I want you to go to the Gonzales Ranch in Southern Mexico," Cassion told the rescue team that was assigned to the recovery of as many of the young men who grew up on Henderson Ranch as possible. "I'm certain you will find several of them on this ranch. Most of them can be taken to one of our facilities near Mexico City. There's one young man in particular I want brought back to Denver. His name is Marco Almanor. There will be several of our people going on this mission with you. Before you land at the ranch, you will be meeting the authorities from the Mexican government. From what we've learned, there will be several arrests made once you get there."

Captain Jules acknowledged the orders of his superior. It seemed strange to think they would be raiding a ranch run by slave labor. How could these people be perpetuating something that was outlawed over two hundred and sixty years earlier?

Along with Captain Jules was his crew, as well as three other rescue mission hovercrafts. He prayed to the One God that he would be able to find the young men who had been sold into slavery before it was too late.

As soon as he landed, the other crafts in his party made their landings. Each of his men took out their laser guns in the anticipation of an armed confrontation.

Three men with rifles stood in front of them.

"We are from the Council of Intergalactic Affairs," Jules announced. "We have been informed you are operating this ranch with slave labor. It is against all of the laws that have been passed in the past two hundred and sixty years."

"You have no right to be on my property," Señor Gonzales said.

"This search warrant gives us the right. We are looking for any men you have working here who are marked as slaves. In particular, we

14

are looking for Marco Almanor. Where is Marco Almanor?"

From the corner of his eye, he saw several men enter the dooryard on horseback. Seeing them made his blood run cold. They were little more than living skeletons. Even from this distance, he could see the electric shock collars around their necks as well as the monitors on their ankles.

"I'm Marco," one young man said as he dismounted, only to immediately collapse.

Thankfully, the medic from Jules' crew was able to catch him before he could slump to the ground.

Attendants from the hovercrafts that landed with him hurried to the sides of the other young men who were with Marco. Each of them was taken to the waiting crafts and one by one they lifted off, out of the reach of Señor Gonzales.

"These men are my property," Carlos shouted. "I paid good money for them. You can't take them away from here."

"You are under arrest," Jules heard someone shout from behind him.

Turning, Jules saw a hovercraft with the insignia of the Mexican government docked across the dooryard. Men in uniform, with their laser weapons drawn, surrounded Gonzales and the men standing shoulder to shoulder.

"Put down your weapons, you are outnumbered and your primitive weapons are of no use to you. You are charged with human trafficking, the perpetuation of slavery, and cruel and inhuman treatment of any and all of the men you have imprisoned on this property. You have the right to remain silent. Anything you say may be used against you in a court of law. You are entitled to a lawyer. If you cannot afford one, one will be appointed to you. Do you understand these rights?"

Gonzales and his henchmen lowered their weapons, a dejected look on their faces. Seeing them in such a state relieved some of the pressure Jules felt earlier about this mission.

"Captain," the medic said, as he came to Jules' side. "This young man is in a critical condition. We need to leave for Denver immediately. We are already starting medical treatment, but until we can get to the facility, it's entirely possible he might not live through the night."

Not knowing what to expect, he'd made certain he had a medical team on board. With the condition of the man he'd just rescued, he prayed they'd be able to keep him alive until they could make it back to Denver.

Around him, the other hovercraft sent by the Council of Intergalactic Affairs took to the air, leaving only the Mexican government personnel to deal with the prisoners they were going to be escorting back to Mexico City.

Once they hit their cruising altitude, he allowed his co-pilot to take over the controls while he went back to check on the patient.

"How is he doing?" he asked the medic.

"It doesn't look good. I've started an IV so we can start getting him some hydration. Once he stabilizes, we can start some nutrients as well."

"Will he make it back to Denver?"

"He will, if we don't encounter any delays. I've been in contact with the clinic at the complex and they assure me that as soon as we dock, they will be able to take him to ICU. It's going to be touch and go but we should be able to make it."

Jules sat for a moment next to the bed where Marco lay. It was possible the young man was dying right before his eyes.

*Dear Father, the One and Only God, watch over this young man and keep him safe as we make this journey to our destination. Don't let him die without getting a chance to live.*

~ * ~

The flight from the southern Nevada base had been three hours long. With the time they'd been on the ground at the Gonzales Ranch they wouldn't arrive back in Denver until the early morning hours.

Going back to the controls, Jules relieved the co-pilot of his duties so he could get some rest. The flight should be relatively routine and he needed the time at the controls in order to compose his thoughts regarding the situation he'd found when he arrived at the isolated ranch.

*How could anyone treat people so inhumanly? At least the shock collar that had been around Marco's neck when we first arrived, as well as the ankle bracelet, were removed before we took off. With them on we would have been unable to transport the young man safely.*

The hours of the flight passed quicker than Jules anticipated. It was three in the morning when they finally arrived at the complex in Denver.

Medical personnel were waiting for them as soon as they were able to safely leave the craft. Everything seemed to move at warp speed. The last Jules saw of Marco was the personnel in medical garb rushing him inside the facility.

After he finished going through the operations to secure his hovercraft, Jules made his way into the complex and the quarters he would be utilizing until he was sent on yet another mission.

"Jules, I hear your mission was a total success," Cassion greeted him.

He looked up at his superior officer. "If you call seeing humanity at its worst a success, I guess it was. I didn't get to see the living quarters for those men, but the condition they were in was enough to turn my stomach. It's only by the grace of the One God that we were able to get our patient here safely."

"I've already been briefed by the other pilots as to what they found at the Gonzales ranch. I'm afraid we've only uncovered the tip of a very large iceberg. Our research has found another ranch, deep in the Yucatan, where there are even more slaves being held. As we speak our men are raiding that place."

"How many more hell holes are we going to uncover? This one was worse than the one in Nevada. I can't imagine what the others could be like."

"For now, you don't have to, my friend. You've earned a reprieve from the missions like the one you just completed. Both you and your crew will have a month's leave coming to you. I know you're anxious to see your wife and kids. I anticipated this and had them brought here early yesterday morning. They're waiting for you in your apartment. I've also ordered the morning meal to be served to you there so you can have some private time. We'll talk more tomorrow after you have time to rest up from this mission."

# Chapter Four

Strange dreams permeated Marco's subconscious. In them he was again with Christopher and his friend was talking to him, telling him he was going to be well again soon. He also dreamed of his mother.

*"We have to be careful,"* she cautioned. *"No one must know who we are. Tell no one your name is Paco. For the rest of your life, you must be Marco and I must be Tessa."*

The dreams seemed to dissipate as quickly as they came, allowing his body the rest it so desperately needed.

~ * ~

Marco could feel awareness returning to his body. For some reason, he thought he'd felt Christopher's presence but he knew that was impossible. He didn't even know if Christopher was dead or alive. Had Henderson sold him to another abuser in the same way as he'd done to the men he worked with at Gonzales' ranch? He hoped not, but he wouldn't put anything past Henderson.

He remembered the last conversation he'd had with Christopher. At that time, he'd told his friend about the group run by Patrick Ernst. Had he been able to make it to Idaho, wherever that was, to join up and start a new life? As soon as the memory crossed his mind, he remembered Mr. Henderson as being the one who told him about Patrick Ernst. Had Christopher been sold to Ernst as he had been to Gonzales?

"Marco, can you hear me?"

The voice was that of a man, but he didn't recognize it as anyone from the ranch. With great difficulty, he opened his eyes. Instead of seeing the bunkhouse, he had no idea where he was. The man who was talking to him didn't look at all familiar. Even sitting in the chair beside where

Marco slept, it was evident he was very tall, with the most piercing violet-colored eyes he'd ever seen.

"Where am I? Is Gonzales coming to take me back to the ranch? I have work to do and…"

The man in the chair silenced him with a wave of his hand. "You are in a hospital, far away from that hell hole where you have been living. Gonzales is in the custody of the Mexican government. That's enough for you to know. For now, your job is to get the proper nutrition and regain your strength."

"What about the others?"

"They're being cared for at other facilities."

"Do you know anything about my friend, Christopher?"

"He is the reason you are here. You will see him soon enough and everything will be made clear. I sent him back to his apartment with strict orders that he is to rest. Tomorrow will be soon enough for the two of you to reconnect and have time to talk."

Although he wanted to ask more questions, Marco could feel his strength waning and gave in to sleep.

~ * ~

Marco sat up in bed for the first time. It amazed him at how much strength it took to accomplish that one small task.

When his meal was brought to him, he wondered how he would be able to eat. He was still considering how he would get the food from his plate to his mouth when a young woman came to his bedside.

"I'm Kara. Dr. Gratan sent me to help you eat."

"No one's ever fed me, at least not that I remember."

"Nonsense. You are just getting your strength back. I am a nurse here at the hospital and it's my job to help you regain your strength. Until last night we weren't sure if you would ever wake up."

Carefully, she tucked a towel into the neck of the hospital gown he wore and spooned broth into his mouth. It seemed strange to taste the rich broth that was in direct contrast to the swill he'd been eating for most of his life.

Once he finished the broth, she reached for a container. It held some substance he didn't recognize. The first spoonful he tasted was sweet and of a different consistency than the broth. He had no idea what she was feeding him, but he knew he liked it.

"What is this?" he asked.

"Haven't you ever eaten applesauce before?"

He shook his head. "What's it made of?"

The look on her face was one of disbelief. "Don't you know what an apple is?"

He decided his look of bewilderment gave her the answer she wanted.

"Apples are a fruit that grows on trees. Some of the best apples have been cultivated here at the complex. Once they are ripe, they can be eaten raw or cooked with sugar to make applesauce."

Sugar was another word that wasn't in his vocabulary. Growing up, nothing that was served at the ranch was sweet like this wonderful concoction Kara called applesauce.

"If you are able to tolerate these soft foods, Dr. Gratan says you will be ready to start eating regular food soon."

With his hunger satisfied, he appreciated Kara lowering the head of his bed so he could go to sleep. It seemed impossible that he was still so tired, but everyone assured him it was part of his healing.

~ * ~

The next time Marco awoke, he lingered in the murky time between sleep and full awareness. This time he was certain he'd heard Christopher's voice. Opening his eyes, he found more mature version of his childhood friend sitting next to the bed. Although they'd seen each other only two years earlier, Christopher's body seemed to have filled out and the haunted look in his eyes now was more confident.

"Christopher," Marco said, his barely audible voice weak. "I couldn't believe it when they told me you were here. I thought I dreamed it."

"I met the hovercraft when they brought you in. It's a long story, but I'm no longer called Christopher. I shortened it to Chris. I did some research and the English version of your name is Mark. For reasons I'll go into later, I think it's best if you start using it."

Confusion crowded Marco's mind. "Why do you think this is good?"

"When I made the decision to change my name, it was because I was about to embark on a new life. Christopher, like Marco, was a child. Chris is who I am today, just as you are Mark. It's best to make a complete break with the past."

Mark nodded. It was best if he changed his name to Mark. In reality it should have been Paco or Frank, but no one needed to know about the secret his mother insisted should never be shared.

"It makes sense. What happened to you after you left the ranch? Did you find Patrick's group?"

"I wanted to ask you about that. How did you hear about them?"

Mark yawned broadly. He couldn't understand why he was so tired when all he wanted to do was to talk to his friend.

"We don't have to talk about this now," Chris suggested. "Think about it and we'll talk more after you get some rest. I won't be going anywhere. This is where I live now."

"At the hospital?" Mark asked, as he was slipping off to sleep.

"Not at the hospital. This is a complex built by the Aliens. I know that's something else that will need explanation."

Although he heard what Chris was saying, he made no attempt to acknowledge it to his friend. Sleep seemed to be the most important thing at the moment.

~ * ~

When Marco again awoke, he thought about what Chris told him earlier. Changing his name wouldn't erase the past, but he understood the necessity of it. As Marco he would always be reminded of where he came from. Mark would give him a new lease on life. It was what he needed.

Opening his eyes, he became fully aware of his surroundings. Chris was sleeping in the chair next to his bed. As much as he wanted to ask the many questions crowding his mind, he was reluctant to interrupt the rest his friend needed.

"Are you awake?" Chris' question came as a surprise.

"I thought you were sleeping."

"Not sleeping, just resting my eyes. Hopefully, you had a good nap."

"I did. I remember you asking me how I knew about Patrick Ernst's group. You did ask me that, didn't you?"

"I didn't think you heard me, but yes, I did ask you that."

"It was Mr. Henderson who told me to tell you about them. He said you weren't cut out to work on any of the ranches in Mexico. He told me you'd do better with a group like his."

"I thought that might be the case. I did join them and I thought it was the best thing I could do. I raised up through the ranks quickly. It wasn't until we came to protest against the aliens here that I realized what we were doing was wrong. We were here with our weapons, ready to fight to the death. I saw two of the recruits, who I'd trained, get killed. Once we came into the complex to meet with their leaders, I was told the truth about the ideals we were fighting for. Suddenly, they didn't seem as important as Patrick told us they were. I also realized the superior race he kept talking about didn't include me. I have Native American blood, just like you come from a Mexican heritage."

"In that group, did they treat you right?"

"They didn't beat me if that's what you mean. The food was a step up from what we got at the ranch. They did feed us three times a day, but only because they needed us to keep up our strength for all the training we did. It wasn't the best food, but at least it wasn't the crap we grew up eating. What I finally realized was that if they'd known about my Native American blood, they would have killed me outright. Thank God, I came here. These people have saved my life. They've also given me the education we were deprived of when we were kids."

"What kind of education?" Mark asked.

"Reading, writing, mathematics, history, geography and science. You have no idea how much it has changed my life."

As much as Mark wanted to ask more questions, he closed his eyes for just a second and immediately slipped into a deep sleep.

# Chapter Five

Each time Mark awoke, he found he was stronger. He looked forward to seeing either Chris or Kara at his bedside.

Slowly, he was told of the events surrounding his rescue from the Gonzales Ranch. The first thing he was told was how the team who brought him to the complex in Colorado were able to remove not only the ankle monitor but also the shock collar before they loaded him into the hovercraft.

Little by little, he came to grips with the terrifying life he'd lived on the Gonzales Ranch. No matter how many questions everyone seemed anxious to receive answers to, he knew there were many things he would never talk about. How could he ever explain the sexual and physical abuse he'd endured over the months he'd been a slave? Just like the name of Paco, it had to remain a secret never to be divulged.

This morning he'd allowed Kara to help him with a sponge bath and now, wearing a clean gown, he waited for Dr. Gratan to come for his early morning visit.

"You look better every time I see you, Mark," Dr. Gratan greeted him.

"I feel better each time I wake up. This morning Kara brought me the most delicious thing I've eaten in a long time. She said it was scrambled eggs. I've never had them before."

Dr. Gratan shook his head in an expression of dismay. "I'm certain there are many things you've never eaten before that you will be trying over the next few weeks. For today, I'd like to have you start your physical therapy."

"Physical therapy?" Mark questioned.

"You have been in this bed for a long time, regaining your strength. Today you are going to get up and start walking."

Mark looked at the doctor, a feeling of confusion encompassing his entire being. He could recall how weak he'd been when he worked on the ranch. There were times he wondered if his legs would support his weight when he dismounted from his horse.

"I-I don't know. Do you think I'm strong enough?"

"I do. It will be hard at first, but you'll do just fine."

Mark took a deep breath before swinging his legs over the side of the bed. That simple action made his head spin, making his confidence drain quickly.

"Not so fast, my boy," Dr. Gratan cautioned. "You've been inactive for a long time. Just sit there for a minute and get your bearings. This being the first time you're out of bed, I want you to use a walker."

Dr. Gratan no sooner spoke the words when Kara appeared with a strange looking metal device with wheels on the front two legs. There were handles on what looked like a cage that would go around his body. For a moment he felt as though he was back at Gonzales Ranch and being put into the cage with no room to even turn around as a punishment.

He pushed the negative thoughts to the back of his mind. These people had been nothing but good to him. Over and over again, they assured him he was safe with them. Even Chris told him he was safe and a new life stretched ahead of him.

With the anxiety relegated to the further most reaches of his conscious thoughts, he focused on the task at hand. Tentatively, he put his feet on the floor and grabbed the bars of the walker, hoping to be able to do what Dr. Gratan expected of him.

The first steps were slow, merely one foot in front of the other, then miraculously, the long-lost strength began to return. He knew he was moving slowly, but he felt as though he was running the way he had when he was a child and still allowed to participate in childhood games.

~ * ~

Within a matter of days, Mark found himself walking the halls of the hospital by himself. After the first day, he'd worked hard to be ready to walk without the walker. Now he found he enjoyed walking the halls of the hospital and spending time in the solarium enjoying the bright sunshine that came through the windows and skylights.

In the evenings, Chris and a young Alien woman named Melian came to his room and started him on the path to getting the education he'd been denied.

It was evident that Melian was as special to Chris as Kara was becoming to him. The emotion radiating from his friend's eyes was evident to Mark even in his weakened condition. It was the love Kara spoke about when they had time to be alone together. The love she told him her parents shared and demonstrated during her childhood. He remembered love. His mother loved him, that was the reason she'd taken him far away from Arizona and changed his name. She loved him so much she wanted to protect him, even if it took her life in the bargain.

"How could you have learned so much in such a short period of time?" Mark asked, when they finished their lesson for the night.

"I don't know, it just happened. I was talking to Cassion and he has made arrangements for you to have an apartment next to mine. Dr. Gratan says you will be released from the hospital in the next couple of days and you'll need a place to live."

"Apartment?" Mark questioned. "I have no idea what you're talking about."

"I didn't either. You'll have a lot to get used to. I went from living in the dorm to the camp in Idaho. As I see it, you went from the dorm to the bunkhouse on the ranch in Mexico. Having a place all to yourself will take some getting used to. Each apartment has a bedroom, bathroom and living room. There's no need for a kitchen, because we take all of our meals in the dining room."

"Let's change the subject," Mark suggested. "What happened to all the children that were at the ranch?"

Mark watched as Chris cringed at his question. "There was a raid on the ranch and the children were all taken to one of the facilities the aliens have around the country. At least most of them were. They found at least fifteen bodies buried behind the box. They haven't told me if they've found more bodies and I don't think I want to know."

"What has happened to Mr. and Mrs. Henderson?"

"They were arrested and there will be a trial soon. I think they are waiting until more of the children have recovered enough to testify against them. I'm ready whenever the trial is held, but the thought of facing those people again makes me very anxious."

Mark understood Chris' apprehensions. He, too, could be called upon to give testimony. He prayed it would be of help in sending the Hendersons to prison for the rest of their lives.

Before Mark could ask any more questions, the alien woman he'd met named Hodia entered the room. "I need to talk to you, Chris," she said.

Chris and Mark exchanged glances, each wondering what could be so important to interrupt their time together. She left the room and Chris followed her.

For a moment, Mark wanted to follow them, but whatever it was Hodia wanted to talk to Chris about was not something that concerned him.

~ * ~

On the morning Mark was released from the hospital, it was Chris, along with Melian and Kara, who took him to the apartment he'd been promised. It was located on the same floor as the one Chris occupied. The ride to the fifteenth floor on the elevator, although frightening, was also exhilarating.

"Just press your hand on this pad," Chris instructed. "It will open the door."

Like an excited child, Mark pressed his hand onto the pad. As he did, the door slid open. Inside was the most luxurious room he'd been in since the night the social worker took him away from the apartment he shared with his mother.

"I can't believe this is all for me," he said, rubbing his hand over the buttery-smooth leather couch.

"You can believe it," Melian assured him. "Chris didn't think he would adapt to having his own apartment, but I'm sure he's told you how much he enjoys his privacy."

"Just think how nice it will be for the two of us to meet here without the doctors, nurses and aides interrupting us whenever we are together," Kara added.

Mark smiled at the thought. He did have feelings for Kara and the thought of exploring them further intrigued him more than he thought possible.

After checking out the bedroom and bathroom, there was a knock at the door. He wondered who it could be, since, other than his companions, he'd made no friends at the complex.

"Cassion and Hodia request permission to be admitted," the automated voice that scared Mark announced.

It was Chris who opened the door for the aliens to enter the apartment.

"I am glad to see you are getting settled in your apartment. We have been doing some research and we'd like to talk to you, if we may."

"Would you like us to leave?" Chris asked.

"No, because what we have uncovered will be of interest to you as well as Mark."

Mark led the way into the living room and took one of the chairs. With Kara sitting in the other chair, Chris and Melian seated themselves on the loveseat, leaving the couch for Cassion and Hodia.

"As Chris knows, I am expert in looking into DNA," Hodia began. "We were surprised to find that you were never chipped, Mark. One of the tests we did was for DNA. We hoped to find out more about your background. What we learned was very interesting."

Mark could feel the uncertainty beginning to rise like bitter gall in his throat. "What did you find?" he finally managed to ask.

"We found there was no name of Almanor in your background. We did find your mother's DNA and her name was Constance Montenegro."

Mark nodded his head. "That was a secret. No one was supposed to know about it."

"Can you tell us about your mother?"

"I was very young when we ran away from our home in Arizona. My mother told me that the bad man who lived there was mean to her and we had to get away from him. She told me her name was now Tessa Almanor and my name was Marco."

"Do you know who this bad man was?"

Ashamed, Mark nodded his head. "He was my father's father. My mother and I went to live there when my father went to prison for hitting my mother. My grandfather was as cruel as my father and my mother said we had to get away before he killed her."

Cassion and Hodia exchanged knowing glances. "That explains a lot," Hodia said. "I have more research to do. I'll keep you informed as to what I find out."

With that, they excused themselves from the group and left the apartment.

"What was that all about?" Chris questioned.

Mark thought about his answer. Chris had been his friend for over sixteen years of his life. Together they'd survived the horrors of growing up on Henderson Ranch. Maybe it was time he told his friend the entire truth.

"I was very young when my father went to prison. I was almost four when we ran away and went to Nevada. My real name was Paco. I guess I was too young to know what my last name was. Since my parents were never married. I assume my mother's family didn't approve of their living together."

"I can understand that," Chris said. "It's the reason my parents were running away when they had the hovercraft accident. I guess it doesn't matter much what your background is, kids think their way of life is the best, no matter what their parents want them to do."

Over the years, Mark had heard the story of Chris' parents and how they both died within hours of each other. It was exciting to know his friend's story had been confirmed after he came to live at the compound.

"Before you ask, I have no idea what my father or grandfather's first or last names were. They were just Papa or Grandfather. The night before we left Arizona, Grandfather was in a rage. My father had been sent to prison and he blamed my mother because she went to the authorities when Papa beat her. That night, Grandfather beat her, just like I'd seen my papa do. When he finished, he left the house. Mama said he went out to go drinking.

"Mama packed a bag with our belongings and stole money out of Grandfather's safe. We left and never looked back. When we arrived in Nevada, Mama told me her name was going to be Tessa and I was going to be Marco. I was never to tell anyone who we really were."

"Did your grandfather beat you?" Kara asked as she wiped the tears from her eyes.

"I think he wanted to, but Mama wouldn't let him, at least not until the night we ran away. Everything went wrong when I got up one morning and Mama wouldn't wake up. I was hungry and wanted her to fix me something to eat. I tried to wake her up a lot of times, but she wouldn't wake up. I don't know why I went outside in the middle of the night but I didn't know what else to do.

"A police officer took me back up to the apartment and went in to check on Mama. He made me stay in the hall. When he came back, he told me a nice lady would come and get me. I went with her but I wanted my mama. After I was with the lady for a while, Mr. Henderson came and got me. From there on, you know what happened to me."

"So, what is your real name?" Chris pressed.

"It was Paco, but I have no idea who that is. I've been Marco for more years than I was ever the scared little boy who couldn't wake up my mama."

"Now, you're Mark," Melian said, after she wiped the tears from her eyes. "It doesn't matter who you were over twenty years ago. Today you're a young man who is seeking not only an education but his future. Everyone here will become your family, just as they have for Chris."

They talked for about an hour before they went down to the dining room to enjoy the evening meal.

With dinner finished, Mark and Chris bid the girls goodnight and made their way to the elevator bank that led to their apartments.

"Do you think you'll be all right by yourself tonight?" Chris asked as Mark opened the door.

"I think so. It's something I've longed for all my life. I gave up looking for monsters under the bed a long time ago. There were enough monsters in my life by the light of day. Night was the only time I knew they couldn't harm me."

# Chapter Six

Mark never though his life could be so perfect. He enjoyed the classes he was attending and was beginning to make plans for the future. He knew he was good with animals, and he decided he would look for a position on a ranch, one that paid their hands and didn't hold them as slaves, forcing them to work from dawn to dusk without adequate food to eat.

At long last they were told they would be going to Virginia City, Nevada to testify at the trial for Theodor and Celine Henderson.

Throughout the morning of the trail, Mark listened to the testimony of Chris as well as many of the other younger boys. He could tell the youngsters were terrified to be in the same room with the Hendersons. Mark decided he would not let the monsters who dominated his nightmares intimidate him.

"State your name," the prosecuting attorney instructed.

"Marco Almanor," he said.

Even though he knew it was a lie, it was the name he had lived with ever since he was four years old. Other than the name Paco, he knew nothing more. It was better that he be identified as he had been for well over sixteen years.

"How did you come to live at Henderson Ranch?"

"My mother and I were living in an apartment in Nevada. One morning she wouldn't wake up. I finally found a policeman and he said she was dead."

"What about your father? Wasn't he with you?"

"No, it was just my mama and me. I was sent away with a lady they said was a social worker. Since I didn't have any family, Mr. Henderson came and took me to his ranch. I thought it was going to be a good place to live, but I was mistaken."

Through the questions the prosecutor asked, Mark's answers mirrored those of Chris and the others who testified perfectly. Even the questions asked by the defense attorney did nothing to shake the story Mark had to tell.

The defense presented its case, with the Hendersons declaring their innocence and describing life on their ranch as a paradise for the young boys no one wanted in their lives.

Once they finished their testimony, the jury was dismissed to come to a conclusion as to guilt or innocence of the monsters who were on trial.

It took a moment for what just occurred to sink in. As he came to grips with the lies his former caregivers told, he saw Chris' ruddy complexion turn deathly pale as he made his way to the rest room.

Mark watched as Chris' Uncle George followed closely behind his friend. By the time they returned to the courtroom, people were already leaving.

While the other boys were taken away by the people who brought them there earlier in the day, Mark and Chris accompanied Chris' Uncle George and Aunt Susan to a small restaurant within walking distance of the courthouse.

It came as a surprise when Cassion was there waiting for them to arrive. "You both did well today," Cassion greeted them. "I don't know if I would had been able to testify so confidently without reaching out to do physical harm to those people."

"I guess the fight went out of me with all the punishments I endured," Chris replied. "I'm out of there now and I have a different life. I only want to see justice done. To be truthful, with the correct management, that ranch could be a very profitable business."

"Chris is right," Mark said, joining the conversation. "I know enough about ranching to know a profitable business venture when I see one. They have some good stock out there. I know Mr. Henderson made a good profit by selling his cattle. I wasn't supposed to know that, but I overheard the two of them talking about how much money they made from selling their beeves, as they called them, without having to pay for ranch hands to do the work. I'm also willing to bet they didn't eat the same slop they fed us."

"You have a point," Cassion agreed. "Ever since their arrest, our representatives have been taking over the operation. We've been looking for a buyer for the property. I think it would be a good investment for the right person."

Mark nodded. "If I had the money, I'd be interested in taking over the running of the place."

"That's exactly what we wanted to hear," George said.

"What are you talking about, Uncle George?" Chris inquired.

"The elders of our tribe have been talking to Cassion about the disposition of the Henderson Ranch. Our elders aren't ranchers, but with the correct management, it could bring in a good profit. Until we can get good management in place, some of our younger men will be working there caring for the remaining stock."

"Isn't that quite a long way away from Montana?" Chris inquired.

"In this day and age, distance doesn't mean much. It's not like the old days, when we traveled on horseback, or even those cars from the twentieth and twenty-first centuries. With the hovercrafts we all fly now, it's only a matter of about an hour to get from northern Montana to Nevada. Cassion and I have decided his people along with ours would be able to continue working the ranch for us until Mark is able to take over."

Chris broke into a wide grin. "It sounds like your future is secure, Buddy," he said as he reached across the table to clasp Mark's hand. "Now, if I can decide what I want to do with my life, we'd both be set."

"George didn't mean to leave you out of things," Susan added. "We've been doing our research about both of you. Mark is a natural for the ranch life. With the proper education he will be one of the best ranch managers we could possibly hire. As for you Chris, I have a feeling you want more out of life than working on a ranch. Your grades, as well as your ability to learn everything so quickly means there are so many doors open to you, you'll be able to do anything you want."

"I want to work with kids," Chris admitted.

"I know you do," George replied. "I'm thinking a home for

troubled youth would be something that might interest you and…"

"…and the ranch would be perfect for something like that," Mark interrupted. "Between the two of us, we could help troubled kids and run the ranch at the same time."

Chris nodded his head in agreement. If the ranch had proper management, it could have been the perfect place for kids to live and learn to be the best people they could be.

~ * ~

With the noon meal finished, they returned to the courthouse. Mark's mind raced with the possibility of what the future held for Chris and himself. As much as he wanted to do ranching, he was a little uncertain if he actually wanted to return to the ranch that was the subject of so many of his nightmares.

"I just heard that the jury is back with a decision," the prosecuting attorney advised them. "It looks like you got here just in time."

Mark worried about what the decision of the jury would be. Would they be taken in by the lies told by both Mr. and Mrs. Henderson? Was it possible they believed the prosecution witnesses who testified against them?

He took the seat he'd occupied at the beginning of the trial, with Chris sitting next to him. He watched as Mr. and Mrs. Henderson were led back into the courtroom. As they approached the table where they'd sat in the morning, they looked confident. Before taking their seats, they both turned and glared at the two of them.

"You'll regret this," Mr. Henderson hissed. "Once this farce is over and we're free, you'd better run for your lives."

Before the two of them could sit down, the bailiff entered the room. "All rise."

Conversations ceased as they judge came into the courtroom.

Chris watched as the jury filed back into the room. He wished he could read their facial expressions.

"Have you reached a verdict?" the judge asked.

"We have, Your Honor," the foreperson of the jury said, as she passed a folded piece of paper to the bailiff.

It took a moment for the judge to read what was written on the paper. "Is this the unanimous verdict of the jury?"

"It is, your honor."

"Theodor and Celine Henderson, please stand. It is the unanimous verdict of this jury that you are found guilty on all counts of the inditements. Due to the severity of your crimes, I sentence you to life imprisonment on the penal colony on the far side of the moon."

An audible gasp sounded throughout the room as Mrs. Henderson fell to her knees, sobs coming from her lips. "Noooooo! That can't be right. We're innocent, I tell you. Innocent. Those boys all lied to you. I know they did."

Chris shook with anger. "How could that woman say such a thing?" Chris whispered to Mark.

Before Mark could answer, a matron and a male guard entered the room. Electronic cuffs and leg monitors were attached to the prisoners' wrists and ankles as they were led out of the room.

"What will their life be like?" Mark asked.

It was Cassion who gave them their answer. "I know that penal colony. My cousin is the warden there. Life for them will not be easy. It was set up for punishments for the most heinous criminals. Considering they are charged with slave trafficking, abuse to minors and fifteen counts of murder, I don't envy them the life they will be living. From what I recall, when they say hard labor, they mean it."

Behind them, the boys who also testified against Mr. and Mrs. Henderson, were jubilant in their reaction to the verdict handed down by the judge and jury.

~ * ~

Once the courtroom emptied. Chris accompanied his aunt and uncle back to their home. Although they invited Mark, he decided not to go with them. This was Chris' time with his family, he certainly didn't want to intrude. Besides, he had a lot of thinking to do and more studies to attend to. He was also anxious to see Kara again.

"Marco, Marco Almanor."

Mark turned at the sound of someone calling his name. Although the man looked somewhat familiar, he couldn't put a name to him. He wondered if he should be afraid. Could this possibly be someone attached to either the Hendersons or Señor Gonzales? If so, was his life in danger?

Putting his fear behind him, he addressed the stranger. "Yes, I'm Marco. Do I know you?"

"I'm certain you don't remember me. I'm Jason Culver. I was the officer who found you on the streets of Elko, Nevada. When I heard about this trial, I wanted to come and possibly reconnect with you. I am so sorry for everything you went through. Believe me, when I sent you to social services, I never expected a monster like Theodore Henderson would become involved in your life."

Mark searched his memory. He did recall the young officer who took him into the apartment building and discovered his mother's dead body.

"I do remember you. It was a terrible time in my life. I never knew what really happened to my mother."

Jason nodded his head. "You were too young to be told everything that happened to her. Do you have some time to spend with me? Maybe we could get a cup of coffee."

Mark looked back toward where he'd left Cassion. "I'll ask. Would you mind if my friend Cassion joined us?"

"Mind? Hardly. I'd be honored to meet him. You might not know it, but he's one of the most important leaders of the aliens in our country."

They waited for a moment for Cassion to join them. After the introductions were made, Cassion suggested they go to the coffee shop in the hotel where he, Chris and Mark were sharing a suite. Since Chris left with his aunt and uncle, Mark would be spending the night alone in the second bedroom.

"I've been very interested in the case of the death of Marco's, I mean Mark's, mother. I've read over the medical examiner's report numerous times. I don't believe she died of natural causes. There was so much internal bruising it was possible she was beaten to death long before she succumbed to her injuries. In other words, she was murdered. Is there anything you can tell me about your life before you moved to Nevada? I know you were very young but…"

Jason left the rest of what he was saying unsaid. Mark knew the man was bewildered by the expression on his face. Even without a mirror, he knew Jason's assumption brought about a sadness that confirmed the truth behind his mother's death.

"The lady at the Social Services house told me my mother was dead. I never knew what caused it, but being a little kid, I wouldn't have understood what any of it meant. I only knew I would never see her again."

"Mark doesn't know much about his past. We did a DNA test and learned his mother's true name was Montenegro."

"Montenegro?" Jason questioned. "That name is familiar. After your mother's death, we received a flyer about a missing person named Constance Montenegro. It was put out by a man named Michael Cruz. He said the woman was his daughter-in-law and she had run away with his grandson, Paco."

Mark felt his heart fall to the pit of his stomach. For the first time, he equated his grandfather, the bad man he told Jason about on the night of his mother's death, with the name Michael Cruz.

"He was my grandfather," he confessed. "He's the bad man we were running away from. My real name is Paco, but I don't want either him or my father to ever find me. We left and changed our names because he beat my mother badly. She also stole money from him before we left. I never thought I would ever know his name or have to see him again."

The expression on Jason's face told Mark he was certain Michael Cruz was guilty of murdering Mark's mother.

"Is there any way we can keep my grandfather from finding me?" Mark asked, his question more of a plea than anything else.

"You'll be safe with us," Cassion promised. "We can start proceedings to legally change your name to Mark Almanor. That should keep him from finding you, at least until he can be located and charged with your mother's murder. There is no statute of limitations on murder. He will stand trial."

"What about your father? Did he know about the abuse?" Jason inquired.

"The reason we were living with Grandfather was that my father was in prison for beating my mother. Grandfather blamed her for not having his son with him. He was worse than my father ever could have been."

"What about your mother's family?"

"I can answer that," Cassion replied. "We've been looking for them but it's a common name. It's possible she ran away from home to be with Mark's father. From what we can tell, she was very young and her parents didn't approve of the man she thought she loved above all others."

Jason nodded his head in agreement. "I'll be in touch with whatever information we come up with. It's possible you will be called to testify at the trial, if a trial is held."

Mark watched as Jason left the coffee shop. It had been a trying day. The trial drained him of his energy as much as the life he'd lived before coming to the complex. He realized he wasn't as strong as he thought. He needed to rest before they made the trip back to the complex in the morning.

# Chapter Seven

Kara waited for Mark at the docking station of the complex. Earlier, they'd received a communication from Cassion, alerting them to the fact the events of the previous days drained the strength Mark regained while he'd been hospitalized. Even though Cassion had no medical training, Kara had no doubt about Mark's condition. The effects of his severe dehydration and malnutrition were ones that would plague him for many months if not for the rest of his life.

The announcement was made that Cassion's hovercraft was preparing for docking. Kara felt her heart begin to pound in anticipation of seeing Mark. She prayed Cassion had been over-stating Mark's condition. The last thing she wanted to see was this man who had become so important in her life relapsing.

Her hopes were shattered when Cassion came into the terminal with Mark. The natural color had drained from Mark's face and he leaned heavily on Cassion. An orderly who came with her from the hospital rushed forward with a wheelchair.

"Get him to the hospital, immediately," she ordered. "I will contact Dr. Gratan to be ready to admit him."

If she thought she would hear words of protest from Mark, there were none forthcoming. It was obvious he was well aware of his condition and gave into the exhaustion that consumed his body.

While the orderly rushed Mark away from the terminal, Kara turned to Cassion for answers as to what had happened while they were in Virginia City. Cassion looked tired, as well as concerned.

"We watched the proceedings via telecom. I thought the trial went very well and Mark did a good job on the stand. What happened to bring Mark to the condition he's in?"

"It's a long story. The trial was draining, but what happened after the verdict was read drained him even further. The police officer who found him on the street in Elko when he was only four years old was at the trial. Afterward he asked if we could meet with him. I'm afraid he brought back some very bad memories for Mark. He believes Mark's mother was murdered and suspects his grandfather as being her murderer. His condition deteriorated greatly after that."

"How horrible. Did he know his grandfather?"

"Meeting with the officer, Jason Culver, a lot of buried memories, or should I say nightmares, came back to him. He remembered his mother stealing money from his grandfather after he beat her severely. She took him from Arizona to Nevada and changed their names. He is so fearful of his grandfather, I assured him we would take the legal steps to change his name to Mark Almanor rather than Paco Montenegro or Paco Cruz. He doesn't know if his mother ever gave him his father's surname. According to the missing person's report, his grandfather listed his mother's last name as Montenegro even though he called her his daughter-in-law. I doubt if she ever married Mark's father."

Kara shook her head. How could Mark have lived with the horror his mother lived through? He must have been completely terrified of his grandfather. It was possible he witnessed the abuse his mother suffered at the hands of the man he described as a monster.

~ * ~

Mark knew he was in trouble even before they took off from Virginia City. If the trial hadn't been draining enough, meeting with Jason Culver brought back terrible memories of the man he'd tried to forget for the past sixteen years of his life.

Hearing the name Michael Cruz conjured the image of his grandfather as well as his father. Over the years, they had haunted his nightmares as nameless monsters. Now they were real. The nightmares came to life. Would they be able to find him? Would they seek revenge for the money his mother took from his grandfather's safe when they ran for their lives into the night?

As soon as they docked, Cassion helped Mark make his way into the terminal. Seeing the look of dismay on Kara's face brought to realization just how dire his situation was. He made no protest when the orderly helped him to seat himself in the wheelchair to be wheeled to the hospital.

He wished Kara was walking by his side, but he knew she was talking to Cassion to learn what had transpired while they were in Nevada.

When he arrived at the hospital, Dr. Gratan was waiting for him. "You need to be admitted to the hospital, Mark. This ordeal has taken a toll on your condition."

Mark didn't argue. He'd spent a sleepless night reliving the nightmare of watching his mother being beaten not only by his grandfather but also by his father. Even though he was but a small child, he remembered the police officer coming to the house and taking his father away. He also remembered his grandfather insisting they come and live with him until his father could return home. What a mistake that had been.

When he did sleep, his dreams were dominated by the angry face of his grandfather as the older man beat his mother without showing any mercy. By learning the name of his grandfather and remembering his father's name, his nightmares were coming to life.

Within minutes of arriving at the hospital, Mark had been helped into a gown and an IV was inserted into his left arm. Although Dr. Gratan didn't say what type of medication was being administered, he knew it had been a sedative, as he slipped into a deep and dreamless sleep almost immediately.

~ * ~

"Do you think we should advise Chris about Mark's condition?" Melian said as she and Kara sat in the dining room for the mid-day meal.

"From what Cassion told me, he's spending time with his family in Montana. He needs this time with them. Besides, there is nothing he can do here. Dr. Gratan has sedated Mark and is giving him medication as well as fluids."

"What could have brought this on?"

Kara chewed thoughtfully on her sandwich before answering. "You watched the trial, the same as I did. It was an emotional time for both Mark and Chris. I worried about Mark, knowing what his condition was when he first came here. He's never going to be as strong as he wants to be. After the trial, the police officer who found him when his mother died asked to meet with him. Cassion told me he was able to remember the horrors that sent his mother to Nevada and caused them to change their names. The officer also told him that he'd always felt Mark's mother was murdered. I'm afraid Mark will have to endure more than one trial in his future. If his grandfather, who the officer thinks is responsible for his mother's murder, is apprehended, it's entirely possible Mark will have to testify at his trial as well as the trial for Carlos Gonzales. The horrors he's had to live through for the past sixteen years will not end soon. I just pray he is strong enough to handle everything that is in his future."

Melian made no reply. She wondered how prudent it was not to tell Chris of his friend's condition. She decided Kara probably was right in her assumption Chris was enjoying time with his family. Once he returned to the complex there would be time to tell him what happened with Mark after they parted company.

~ * ~

Mark could not believe how draining the trip to Virginia City had been. He knew the trial for the Hendersons would be difficult, but meeting with Jason Culver left him completely exhausted.

He never expected to hear his mother's death was considered a murder. Over the years he'd only remembered the bad man, but hadn't made the connection with his grandfather until Jason told him about the missing person's report that had been issued about Mark's mother.

As he lay in his hospital bed, he thought about his grandfather. He hadn't brought those memories to mind in years. Why should he? When he and his mother left Arizona, she told him they'd cut all ties and would never have to deal with either his grandfather or his father again. In reality she was right, at least for that moment. What if he had to meet either Michael Cruz or his own father sometime in the future? Thinking of his father brought to mind the officers who arrested him, calling him Stephen. It was possible his father's name was Stephen Cruz. Would he be strong enough to handle such encounters?

From outside his room, he heard a commotion. Praying it had nothing to do with him, he decided to take a nap. Unfortunately, the voices soon became louder, turning into an argument.

"I know you have my nephew here. I've been tracing my sister for many years. Recently, I found out she was missing from Arizona. I read an article about it in the National Reporter about a young woman who had been beaten to death. The article said that she had been identified as Constance Montenegro. It also said her son, Paco, is here under the name of Almanor."

"I'm not at liberty to give you any information," he heard Kara say. "Let me call Dr. Gratan and Cassion. Dr. Gratan is the head of our medical team and Cassion is the administrator of the entire complex."

"Call whoever you want, but I tell you I demand to see my nephew. From what the article said about him and my sister, he has been mistreated for his entire life."

Mark considered the implications of meeting with this man. He'd been too young to remember anything other than the abuse his mother endured at the hands of his father and paternal grandfather. He had no idea why she never spoke of her own family or if they were someone to be feared as well.

"I'm Dr. Gratan."

Mark breathed a sigh of relief. As angry as the man talking to Kara sounded, he knew Dr. Gratan could defuse the situation. He didn't like the idea of her having to confront this man by herself, but he was in no shape to go out and help her, not considering he was hooked up to several IV's and monitors.

"I'm Phillipe Montenegro. Like I told the young lady, I have been searching for my sister Connie for over twenty years. From what I read in the paper, her son is here and goes by the name of Mark Almanor."

"Could I see some identification? The man you are inquiring about is my patient, but he is in a very serious condition. Until I know you mean him no harm, I cannot allow you to see him."

There was a moment of silence, until Mark recognized Cassion's voice, reiterating everything Dr. Gratan just told the stranger who was demanding to be allowed entry into Mark's room.

All thoughts of his fear of Michael or Stephen Cruz left Mark's mind. This new man was an unknown complication to his situation. Would he pose the same threat as his father's side of his family?

Rather than dwell on the what ifs in his life, Mark closed his eyes and drifted off to sleep.

~ * ~

Cassion assessed the man who insisted he was Mark's maternal uncle. Having learned the past history of how the boy's mother died and the part his paternal grandfather played in her death, he worried about allowing this stranger access to Mark's room.

"You have to understand, your nephew is still very weak," Dr. Gratan said, once the three of them were in one of the private offices.

"I don't know or understand anything, other than my sister is dead and her son is being held prisoner here."

Cassion cleared his throat before replying to Phillipe's statement. "There is a lot you don't know about Mark. His past is just now coming to light. I have no idea why your sister wasn't with your family, but from what we can ascertain, Mark's father had been arrested for physically abusing his mother. Since he was in custody, she was living with Mark's grandfather. She stole money from the old man and ran away after he beat her unmercifully. She changed her name to Tessa Almanor and told Mark he would be called Marco rather than Paco. They were living in an apartment in Elko, Nevada when she passed away."

Phillipe help up his hand to silence Cassion's narrative. "If she told him his name was Marco Almanor, why are you calling him Mark?"

46

"If you would allow me to finish, I think you will understand. Mark was about four years old and found wandering in the street in the early hours of the morning. He told the officer who found him that his mother wouldn't wake up and he was hungry.

"When Officer Culver went into their apartment, it was evident she'd been dead for several hours. Mark was turned over to social services and, with no close relatives, he was sent to a ranch for unwanted children."

"Henderson Ranch," Phillipe interrupted. "Who in their right mind would send a child to that hell hole? I read about the trial and the atrocities that were perpetuated there."

"Mark was one of the young men who testified against them. You have to remember that was sixteen years ago and at the time no one knew what was going on other than they were caring for orphaned and unwanted children.

"It was when one of the boys who had been at the ranch with Mark came here with a militant group to protest that anyone started to look into what was going on out there. I'm proud to say that I was the person responsible for the raid on that property as well as the liberation of the younger boys still in their care. When we made the raid, we learned more about what happened once the children aged out of the program.

"From the information Chris, the first young man to be identified, gave us, we learned about how many of the boys were working in Mexico. It was imperative for Chris to find out about Mark, who had been one of his best friends while growing up. I won't sugarcoat anything—when our people rescued Mark, no one knew if he would live long enough to make it here so he could get proper medical care."

"How could that be? I have relatives who have ranches in Mexico and I've always considered it to be one of the healthiest lifestyles anyone could live."

Cassion ached for Phillipe. It was hard enough to find a nephew you thought was lost and then to try to comprehend the conditions Mark endured for sixteen years of his young life.

"When Mark aged out of the program, Henderson took him into

Mexico and sold him as slave labor on a remotely located ranch. He was suffering from malnutrition and dehydration when he got here. As for the name change, that was Chris' idea. He told us that, as Christopher, he was a frightened child and since he was starting a new life, he wanted to be called Chris. He made the same suggestion to Mark when he came. Mark was receptive to changing his name from Marco, because as Chris told him, Christopher and Marco were slaves for most of their lives and they needed to put the past behind him."

"From what you just said, Connie named him Paco. Why not go back and use that name?"

"Let me finish and you will understand more." Cassion could feel his patience wearing thin with Phillipe's constant interruptions.

"After the trial for the Hendersons was held in Virginia City, Officer Culver approached Mark and myself. He said he was the officer who found Mark wandering on the street and was the first one to find your sister deceased. He never forgot the case, because after Mark was sent to Henderson Ranch, the autopsy showed his mother died from massive internal injuries caused by the beating she took at the hands of Mark's grandfather. It wasn't until the officer heard of the trial and came in the hopes of seeing the boy he'd rescued so many years earlier that he put two and two together. He remembered receiving a missing person's report for Constance Montenegro and her son, Paco. It was issued by Michael Cruz.

"From the combination of the trial and meeting Officer Culver, I could see Mark's health beginning to take a turn for the worst. When we got back to our hotel, he begged me to help him have his name legally changed to Mark Almanor and I agreed. I knew it would keep him safe from the grandfather who had beaten his mother to death."

"What is being done about Michael Cruz?"

"Officer Culver assured me he would be swearing out a warrant for the man's arrest for murder. He said he would be keeping us apprised of any arrest that is made. It's possible Mark will have to testify at that trial as well as the one for the rancher in Mexico. We are all concerned about his health. Rather than being a prisoner here, he is in our protective care. Dr. Gratan, as well as Nurse Kara, is taking good care of him and many of the instructors here are helping him with his educational needs."

Phillipe hung his head and Cassion could see tears rolling down his cheeks.

"This certainly isn't what I expected to hear. I can fill in the gaps in the story as far as my sister is concerned. Connie was dating Stephen Cruz, when one night she never came home. My parents always thought she'd run away with Stephen, since they didn't approve of him. He was older than her.

"I realized she hadn't run away when we had no contact with her once she left. We had a missing person's report out on her in Texas, where we lived, but nothing ever came of it. I was certain he had killed her and hidden her body somewhere no one would find it. He must have gotten her pregnant and told her if she told our parents, they would insist on her getting an abortion. Of course, that's the last thing they would have wanted. They both died not knowing what happened to her. If I hadn't seen the information in the paper, I would have never come here to find him."

Dr. Gratan finally gave voice to his concerns about Mark's health. "The reason I was so guarded about you seeing Mark was because of the condition he was in when he returned to the complex from Virginia City. He was in almost the same condition as when he first arrived. Even though he was no longer suffering from malnutrition and dehydration, the trial and meeting with Officer Culver drained his strength completely. To be truthful, it was too soon in his recovery for him to be under such a stressful situation."

"Will he make a recovery?" Phillipe questioned.

"Yes, but it will be a long time in coming."

"What will he do with his life?"

Cassion smiled at the concern in Phillipe's voice.

"I can answer that. Chris has Native American roots and he has reconnected with people from both sides of his family. The tribe his family is associated with has made an offer to purchase Henderson Ranch and they want Mark to manage it. He was agreeable, as he said he does enjoy ranch work and knows Henderson Ranch could be a profitable investment."

"Mark is not without resources," Phillipe replied. "Our parents were very wealthy and when they passed away, my sister was provided for in their will. I invested her money, in the hopes that one day I would find her and convince her to return to Texas. Her inheritance is there for Mark to do with as he wishes. If being the ranch manager for that property is something he is interested in, my brother and I will be more than willing to help him in any way we can."

"Since that is the case." Dr. Gratan said, "I'll go and check on Mark. If he is receptive to meeting you, I'll come and get you. For now, why don't you and Cassion go down to the dining hall and get something to eat? I'll meet you there a bit later."

Cassion watched Dr. Gratan leave the office before escorting Phillipe to the dining area.

"I hope you're prepared to stay for a few days. I'll have accommodations prepared for you."

"I didn't know what to expect. I was prepared to make reservations in the city."

"Nonsense. There is more than enough room here. We keep apartments for visiting dignitaries from other complexes around the world. We are known to have one of the best medical facilities in the country and many people come here to study under Dr. Gratan. We have physicians both from our people and the Earthly population."

"This is all very overwhelming. I didn't know what to expect. Like I said earlier, I thought Mark was being held prisoner here."

"You have much to learn about our operation. I'd like to know more about you. What is it your family does?"

"My brother, Jonathan, is a veterinarian. He practices in Houston and teaches veterinary medicine at one of the local colleges. I, on the other hand, have taken over our father's position as an investment banker. I've been handling the family finances ever since our parents died. When we learned about our sister and that her son had been brought here, I was the one who could get away to investigate. I'm afraid my brother's position is of the utmost importance and he can't be gone for several days at a time as easily as I can."

Cassion was finding Phillipe to be a very charismatic man, despite the first impression he'd given off when he was demanding to visit Mark.

## Chapter Eight

Dr. Gratan found Kara at the nurses' station outside of Mark's room. Seeing her there, he remembered the earlier confrontation she'd had with Phillipe Montenegro. She'd been wise to call on him as well as Cassion rather than try to handle the situation on her own. The man was someone who was not accustomed to dealing with those he considered below his station in life.

"How is Mark doing?"

"He's been sleeping since just after that nasty man who said he was Mark's uncle arrived. Is he someone we should be afraid of? Is he here to do harm to Mark?"

He was pleased with Kara's concern for Mark. It was easy to tell she thought of him in other ways than just another patient. He'd worried about her finding love away from the complex on the far side of the moon where she'd been raised.

"On the contrary," he finally replied. "Phillipe is the brother of Mark's mother. For over twenty years he's searched for her, not knowing where she went. He's like the family Chris found. He wants to embrace Mark as his nephew and reintroduce him to the rest of his mother's family. I've come to talk to Mark about arranging a meeting between the two of them."

As though on cue, the monitor on Kara's desk started to beep, indicating Mark had awakened.

"You don't need to go in there, I'll gladly check on him since we have much to discuss."

From the look on Kara's face, he knew his decision disappointed her. It was evident she desired to spend as much time with Mark as she could possibly have.

"Since we have no other patients, at the moment, why don't you go down to the dining hall and get something to eat. I have seen your dedication and I worry that at times you neglect yourself when you are caring for your patients."

He could see her disappointment turn to anticipation of having some time to herself. He waited until she disappeared behind the doors of the elevator before going into Mark's room. By the look on the young man's face, he was disappointed not to see Kara coming to see how he was doing.

"I was talking to Kara when I saw you were awake," Dr. Gratan began. "Since I wanted to check on you as well as talk to you about something, I sent her down to the dining hall to have her lunch. She tends to forget to take her meals when she's working. I admire her dedication, but she must take care of her health as well."

While Mark made no comment, he nodded his head.

"You had a visitor this morning."

Mark snapped to immediate attention. "I heard what sounded like an argument earlier."

"You heard correctly. Your uncle, Phillipe Montenegro, wanted to see you. He was very argumentative with Kara. Luckily, she was able to contact Cassion and myself. Together we were able to take him to a private area and apprise him of your condition. It turns out he has been searching for your mother ever since she went missing almost twenty-two years ago. I told him the decision for him to meet with you would be yours and yours alone."

"What does he want?" Mark asked.

"He wants to meet you and complete his family. It took a toll on him when I told him about the death of your mother. He was hoping to be able to reconnect with her, even though I'm certain he knew she was no longer living. He did say that her share of the inheritance from their parents has been invested and is there for you, should you decide to make a connection with this side of your family. He certainly means no harm to you, unlike the paternal side of your family."

"That's a lot to digest. I've been alone for most of my life. The thought of having a family is completely alien to me. It will do no harm to meet him. I mean, with everyone here at the complex, I know it will be safe."

"I was hoping that would be your decision. From what I can tell he is sincere. He means you no harm. Cassion has persuaded him to stay here at the complex so the two of you can get better acquainted."

"Can I get out of this hospital bed? I would rather meet him man to man than have him towering over me."

Dr. Gratan took a moment to consider Mark's proposition. "I don't think you are strong enough to stand on your feet for too long, but I have no objections to taking you to a meeting with your uncle in a wheelchair. I'll order something to be brought to you for a meal while Cassion and I make the necessary arrangements."

~ * ~

Cassion was getting better acquainted with Phillipe when he received a communication from Jason Carver in Nevada.

"This is important," he said, excusing himself from Phillipe's company.

Once outside of the office where they'd been meeting, Cassion answered the communication.

"Do you have news?" he asked.

Jason's face filled the screen. "I have very good news. Michael Cruz was arrested this morning. Once we charged Michael with murder, he became very combative. He's in police custody now."

"Was his son with him?"

"No, but he did contact him. It seems as though he thought his son could bail him out of jail. Of course, there is no bail set for him."

"Good. Once you know where Stephen lives, go there and arrest him as well. We have new information that it's possible he kidnapped Mark's mother. They were dating and one night she never returned from their date. I'm sure he thought she would be his to do with as he pleased for the rest of her life. Little did he know she would call the authorities on him when he beat her so severely. It's too bad she was sent to live with his father rather than sending her back to her family in Texas."

"I'm sure there is quite a story behind your accusations. I can hardly wait to hear it. For now, I'd best get busy issuing that warrant for Stephen Cruz's arrest. We'll be in contact later."

The connection was broken. Cassion was about to go back into the room where he and Phillipe had been talking, when he met Dr. Gratan coming from the direction of the hospital.

"Is Mark willing to meet with Phillipe?" he asked.

"He is. I told him I would make arrangements for a meeting between the two of them. He doesn't want to meet his uncle confined to a hospital bed."

"That's excellent news. Before you make those arrangements, you should be told what I just learned from Jason Culver. I received a communication from him saying Michael Cruz, Mark's paternal grandfather, was arrested on the charge of the murder of Mark's mother. I told him to arrest Stephen Cruz on the charge of kidnapping. I think we will be able to lay to rest the ghosts of Mark's past. With the boy meeting his Uncle Phillipe, he will be able to have a brighter future."

~ * ~

Mark was pleased when Kara entered his room carrying a food tray. He welcomed her company more than that of Dr. Gratan.

"It's good to see you awake," she greeted him. "I met Dr. Gratan and he told me to bring you something to eat. I hope you're hungry."

"I'm starved, but not just for the food. I've missed you."

A blush flushed her cheeks. "You flatter me."

"I'm ignorant about a lot of things, but I always tell the truth. That was something the Hendersons beat into me. I missed you when I went back to Nevada. I don't ever want anyone to keep us apart again."

Kara laughed at his declaration. "I think you're delirious from hunger. If it makes any difference, I missed you as much as you missed me. When you came back and were so sick, I was afraid…"

Mark held up his hand to silence her. "I've lived through too much to die now. I've been offered a fantastic opportunity that will secure my future and the future of the ranch where I grew up. I will be able to have a hand in changing it for the better."

Kara sat down the tray on the side table next to the bed. She helped him to sit on the side of the bed in order to be able to eat more comfortably.

With each plate uncovered, Mark could feel his mouth start to water. After all the years of being deprived of edible food, he'd come to enjoy every entry he was served. As much as he wanted to eat everything on the tray, he found even this simple task to be exhausting.

After eating enough to satisfy Kara, he laid his fork down beside the plate. "I never thought eating would take so much strength."

Kara helped him to lie back down on the bed.

"Do you think Dr. Gratan would be angry if I took a nap before I met my uncle?"

"I think he would say it is just what you need. There will be plenty of time for meetings. You need to regain your strength and that is the top priority."

Mark cursed his body's need for rest, but worried about another relapse if he didn't give in to the need. What happened while he was in Nevada scared him. He had no desire for anything like that to happen again.

~ * ~

Kara helped Mark to become comfortable before she picked up the tray of uneaten food so it could be taken back to the kitchen. By the time she was ready to leave the room, Mark was sleeping soundly.

Once she returned to the nurses' station, she activated her communicator and waited for Dr. Gratan to respond.

"Did Mark eat his meal?" Dr. Gratan asked.

"He said he was starving, but in actuality he ate very little of it. It seemed to exhaust him. I think he is looking forward to seeing his uncle, but he needed to sleep more."

"I understand and so will his uncle."

"I hope so. I am not as certain as you are about his recovery from this setback. How could eating a meal be so exhausting?"

There was a pause before Dr. Gratan answered her question. "Have faith, Kara. You must remember the condition he was in when he first arrived. I was against him going back to Nevada, but his presence was expected at the trial. He will regain his strength, but it will not happen overnight."

The connection ended and Kara turned her attention to charting Mark's vitals. Everything looked good, especially the lab work. Perhaps Dr. Gratan was correct, what Mark needed most was rest and she would see to it he received it.

With no other duties to occupy her time, she recalled Mark's proclamation of how he felt about her. She'd fallen in love with him the first time she saw him. Before this she never believed in love at first sight. Things like that only happened in the old romance novels her mother used to read. Now she was rethinking her position.

~ * ~

When Mark again awoke it was dark outside. He knew Kara's shift would be over and another nurse would take her place. He wondered if it was too late for him to meet the uncle who came earlier to find him.

Before he could ring for the nurse, the night nurse entered his room. "I saw on the monitor that you were awake," he said.

It wasn't much of a surprise to see a male nurse, as he'd become acquainted with Lago when he'd been a patient after first arriving.

"Do you think it's too late for me to meet my uncle?" Mark asked.

"It's not as late as you might think, but Dr. Gratan left orders that the reunion shouldn't take place until morning. I've ordered a meal to be sent up for you. According to Kara's notes, you didn't eat much when you were last awake. If possible, I'd like to see you eat more of your meal."

Mark agreed. He was hungrier now than when he'd last awaken. Without Kara to distract his mind, he hoped he would be able to eat more.

He did like having Lago as his night nurse. They were about the same age and he decided he could talk about some of the new feelings he was experiencing with him, easier than he could with Kara.

An orderly brought up the tray with Mark's meal. Again, he was overwhelmed by the amount and the quality of the food he was being served.

"Can you sit and talk with me for a while?" he asked, after finishing the majority of the food he'd been given.

"What do you want to talk about?"

"I'm having some strange feelings when Kara is near me. I told her earlier that I think I love her, but other than the short time I was with my mother, I have no idea what love is."

Lago smiled. "I have been told your story, and I can understand your questions. It was the same when I first met my wife. She was the most beautiful girl I could ever remember seeing. When we had a chance to come to Earth and be part of this complex, we were thrilled. What you are feeling is natural for a young man. You have to remember the females of the species are much different from us men. They are perpetual romantics, where we have urges that make our bodies do strange things."

Mark nodded. He understood exactly what Lago was talking about. When Kara was helping him earlier, he was embarrassed by the way his body reacted. No one ever explained things like this to him when he was in the process of becoming a man.

"I'm pleased to know what happens when I'm around Kara is natural."

"As natural as breathing. You just have to remember not to follow through on any of your urges until you are certain this is the woman you want as your wife for the rest of your life. Women are to be cherished rather than used for our own pleasures."

"I have been having strange dreams about her and when I wake up…"

"You don't have to go any further. What you are experiencing is normal in boys in their early teens. Because of your background, it's no wonder this is happening to you at this stage of your life. I will make it my duty to answer any questions you might have about what you are experiencing. It will give me good practice for when my son is old enough to start asking these same questions."

Mark was relieved. He'd been concerned about these things his body was experiencing. He also knew asking such questions of Kara would be inappropriate.

"You mentioned a wife as well as a son. I thought you were about my age."

Lago smiled at Mark's statement. "I'm about ten years older than you. It's just that our people don't usually show our age. My son is five years old and keeps me young whenever I get to spend time with him. He's very active."

Mark closed his eyes and recalled the carefree days before he turned six and took on the duties and responsibilities meant for men, not boys, to be doing. Just the thought of what he remembered, brought a lump to his throat. He should have been reunited with his mother's family shortly after her death, instead of waiting for sixteen years to meet them.

# Chapter Nine

Phillipe settled into the room that was more like an apartment than a single room at the Alien Complex. His emotions were in knots. From what he'd learned over the past few days his sister Connie was dead and her son Mark wasn't using the family name.

He'd come to the complex certain they were holding his nephew prisoner, only to learn of the boy's troubled past. It saddened him to think Mark's medical condition was so critical he would be unable to even meet him until the next morning.

His communicator indicated an incoming communication. As soon as he activated it, the face of his brother Jonathan filled the screen.

"Did you find him?"

"I did. You aren't going to believe this, Jon. I'm at the Alien Complex in Denver. He's a patient at the hospital here. I think you should get up here as soon as possible. Like we thought, Connie is dead. At the time she died she was running away from Stephen's father. They've arrested the old man for murder and have issued a warrant for Stephen for kidnapping."

"I don't know what to say. What about her son?"

"When Connie died, she was using an assumed name. Since they couldn't find any family, Mark was sent to Henderson Ranch. When he aged out of their program, he was sold, as a slave, to a ranch in Mexico. He's in pretty rough shape, physically. After he testified against the Hendersons last week, he had a relapse. I've been told I'll be able to see him in the morning."

"Are you sure he's actually Connie's son?"

"Positive. After Connie died, the officer who found her came across a missing person's report for her. When all of this stuff with Henderson Ranch came to light, he remembered helping Mark out that night. He was at the trial and Mark told him his real name was Paco, but his mother told him not to use it because of the man he called the 'Bad Man.' They now know that was Michael Cruz, Mark's paternal grandfather."

"I see. As much as I dislike flying at night, I'll make some arrangements here and take the first commercial flight I can get to Denver. Do you think someone can meet me at the docking port?"

"I'm certain the man I met with this morning will be able to go there and pick you up. Keep me apprised of your arrival time. Oh, yes, his name is Cassion. I think he's the head honcho here. He certainly gave me a good grilling when I wanted to see Mark. They're very protective of him as well as the other young man who lives here who was brought up on Henderson Ranch."

"I remember reading about the trial and the two young men from that complex who testified against the Hendersons. It makes me sick to think of anyone having to suffer at the hands of those monsters. It's even worse to think about our nephew being one of the children they abused."

Without further comment, Phillipe ended the connection. He knew he would be much more at ease once Jon arrived.

~ * ~

Jon didn't know what he expected to hear when he talked to his brother, but it certainly wasn't that their nephew had been abused for most of his life. He remembered talking about making the trip to Denver. At the time, his schedule at the clinic had been so busy, he didn't think he'd be able to get away. Now, he regretted his decision. Phil was certain this young man who called himself Mark Almanor was their nephew, Connie's only child.

At the time Connie disappeared, he'd agreed with his father and blamed Stephen Cruz for her no longer being with the family. Now, he knew Cruz took Connie away against her will, or so it seemed. Hearing that Stephen's father had been arrested for her murder, he wanted just ten minutes alone with the two of them. The only problem with his desire would mean he would spend the rest of his life in prison.

As soon as the connection with Phil was ended, Jon let his wife know what was happening. She agreed to pack a bag for him as he made arrangements for a commercial hovercraft flight to Denver.

"Do you know what you'll find when you get there?" his wife Serina asked.

"I don't have any idea. What I do know is if this young man is Connie's son, I'll know it immediately. If it's not, I'll be back home by tomorrow night. Otherwise, I want to see what I, or I should say the family, can do to help him move forward with his life. You read the reports about what happened at Henderson Ranch. Those kids were given inadequate meals to say nothing about being used as slave labor and not being educated. I just can't imagine a situation like that in this day and age."

Within the hour, a shuttle driver arrived at the ranch Jon and Serina called home, in order to take him to the docking port to make his scheduled flight to Denver. The time the flight took to get to Denver would give him time to formulate a plan as to what the family could do to help Mark in the future, if he turned out to be Connie's son, the only link they would ever have to the sister they'd grown up with and loved.

~ * ~

Mark waited for Kara to come into his room to take his morning vitals. After his talk last night with Lago, he was much more comfortable with the feelings he was experiencing for Kara. Knowing what was happening to him was normal made him anxious to further explore his feelings.

"Good morning," Kara greeted him.

He loved the sound of her cheerful greeting. "Good morning to you, too."

"You look much better this morning. Did you rest well last night?"

"I did. Even though I had a lot on my mind, I was able to sleep peacefully."

Before she commented further, she took his vitals and recorded them on the computer positioned next to his bed.

"Everything looks better than it did yesterday. You certainly had me frightened. I talked to Dr. Gratan and Cassion this morning. They told me not only your Uncle Phillipe is here but his brother Jonathan arrived last night. Do you think you're up to meeting your family?"

"Family," Mark repeated. "I remember my mother telling us we were our own family. If she'd lived longer, perhaps I would have met these people sooner than now. Since her death I have been alone for most of my life. I had friends among the kids on Henderson Ranch, but it wasn't the same as family. I have no idea what having a family will be like."

Kara smiled at him, making him wonder if she knew something about his future he didn't know or even comprehend.

A knock at the door signaled the arrival of his breakfast. Even though he had no idea what was on the tray, he could feel his stomach growling in anticipation of the morning meal.

"Do you think you'll need help eating your breakfast?" Kara asked.

"Probably not, but if you don't have any pressing duties, I'd enjoy your company while I eat. I don't think I've ever eaten a meal without someone else with me."

"I promised Dr. Gratan I would make certain you ate everything on your tray."

At Kara's insistence, he moved from his bed to one of the chairs in the room. It felt good to be sitting in a chair rather than to be trying to eat a meal while in bed.

While he ate, Kara busied herself with changing the bedding, checking his IV bags and getting out a set of scrubs.

"What, no gown?" he teased.

"If you're going to meet your family, I think you would feel better about it if you were wearing scrubs rather than a gown. Besides, Dr. Gratan will be here soon and if your labs and other numbers are stable, he may discontinue the IV. If he does that, you won't need to wear the gown. The scrubs will be more suitable."

~ * ~

Phil and Jon enjoyed the morning meal they shared in the dining hall. They were just finishing when Cassion came to join them at their table.

"I trust your accommodations were suitable," he greeted them.

"They were, thank you," Jon replied. "Have you heard if our nephew is up to having company?"

"I just spoke with Dr. Gratan and Mark's nurse, Kara. They are both pleased with the progress he has made since he returned from Nevada. The trial there, as well as the meeting with Justin Culver, were very draining for him. They both fear it was too soon after he had been rescued from the ranch in Mexico for him to be undergoing the stress of the trial. He is anxious to meet the two of you as well. He wanted to meet you last night but Dr. Gratan felt the time wasn't right."

Phil let out a sigh of relief. "I have to admit, I put in an anxious night. I was afraid he wouldn't want to see us, since we were unable to protect him and his mother."

"On the contrary. He had no idea either of you even existed. You must remember he was only four at the time of her death. He grew up doing and seeing things that sometimes weren't beneficial for children to see, to say nothing of knowing about. Even if he did know about his mother's family, there has been so much trauma in his life it could be buried deeply in his subconscious."

"I'm a little late getting in on this, but are you certain the young man is actually our sister's son? I mean, at this late date, he could say anything."

"We've checked his DNA chip and I'm certain if we check it against your DNA it will prove to be a match."

"I've been praying that would be the case. It's been over twenty-two years since our sister disappeared. I never thought we would find her, to say nothing about finding she had a child. I'm certain I am as anxious to meet him as you say he is to meet us."

~ * ~

Mark felt completely refreshed after taking his shower and dressing in clean scrubs. Dr. Gratan removing the IV from his arm was an added bonus.

"Are you ready to meet your family?" Cassion said as he entered the room.

"I was ready last night, but I think Dr. Gratan was right, I needed a good night's rest to be ready for this reunion."

Cassion smiled at his reply.

Mark watched him leave and held his breath in anticipation of meeting the two men who proclaimed to be his family. Would they be as abusive as his grandfather, the Hendersons, and Señor Gonzales had been, or would they be loving as he remembered his mother being? Only time would tell.

The door opened again and two men entered the room. The strong resemblance to his memory of his mother left no doubt about them being his family.

The younger of the two men was the first to approach the chair where he was sitting. "Don't get up," he said. "I'm your Uncle Phillipe but everyone calls me Phil."

Mark shook his uncle's hand. As hard as he tried, he couldn't restrain the tears that threatened to run down his cheeks uncontrollably.

"I'm your Uncle Jonathan, but like Phil I prefer to be called Jon. Your mother was our younger sister. We've wondered what happened to her for over twenty years. I certainly don't need a DNA chip to tell me you're Connie's son. I can even see some of your father's features in you."

"You knew him, my father, that is?" Mark managed to say.

"Phil knew him better than I did, because the two of them were in the same class in school. Connie was three years younger than they were and she fancied herself in love with him. When she told our father, they were in love and wanted to get married, he forbade it. The next day both Stephen and Connie disappeared. Since Connie was underage, Papa was certain Stephen kidnapped her. Of course, he couldn't prove it."

"I don't remember much about him," Mark admitted. "Mama told me I was only three years old when she called the police on my father for beating her. She said my grandfather insisted we come and live with him while my father was away. I thought he was a monster because he beat my mother just like my father did, or at least that's what she told me. That was why she stole the money from his safe and we ran away."

"When the police officer found you, why did you tell him your name was Marco Almanor? Why not tell him your real name?"

"Mama said I should never tell anyone what my real name was because if the monster found out where we were, he'd come and hurt us again."

Jon dropped to one knee to be on eye level with Mark. "Did Michael Cruz hurt you?"

Mark's mind spun back to the night before he and his mother left the Cruz home. He remembered the monster hitting his mother and knocking her to the floor. In his memory from over sixteen years ago, he screamed, "Don't hurt my mama."

In retaliation, the monster hit him so hard across his face that he flew across the room. Something warm and wet ran from his nose and down his lip. It was then the monster threw a cloth at him and told him to shut up and clean up the mess he made.

Tears flowed faster at the memory.

"Did you hear me?" Jon asked. "Did that old man hurt you?"

Unable to form the words, Mark nodded his head. Finally, he willed his tears to quit falling. "Not as bad as he hurt my mother. I remember blood flowing from my nose and him telling me to clean it up. After it happened, we left the house. At that time, my mother and I ran away with the money she stole. That was why she told me never to tell anyone our real names."

He raised his head, no longer shamed about the reason they'd run away. Telling someone the story lifted any guilt either he or his mother once had. When he did, he saw both of the men who signified his family wiping tears from their faces as well.

"Ten minutes, that's all it would take," Phil swore. "If I had ten minutes I could…"

"No, you couldn't," Mark interrupted him, surprising himself by how mature the words coming from his mouth sounded. "I thought that was what I wanted with the Hendersons. At the trial, I realized it was best to let the courts deal with them. Taking the law into my own hands would make me no better than they were. It will be the same when that monster as well as Señor Gonzales go to trial. Hopefully, by the time those trials are held, I'll be strong enough to handle it."

"You certainly are your mother's son," Phil said. "She was always the most level-headed of all of us. My temper always used to get me in a lot of trouble. It was the same with you, Jon."

Mark looked at his older uncle. He could tell by the look in Jon's eyes that he wanted to argue with Phil, but it wouldn't do any good. As a child, he'd let his temper get the best of him once and it cost him a six hour stay in 'the box.' It didn't take long for him to realize anger and temper tantrums would get him nothing but punishment in this life.

"Do you think you'd like to come to Texas and stay with us?" Jon asked.

Mark thought about it for a moment before answering. "I'd like to come for a visit, but I've been offered a good opportunity."

"What kind of opportunity?" Phil asked.

"My friend, Chris, has Native American blood and that side of his family has offered to purchase Henderson Ranch. They would like me to help them manage it. I'm good at ranching and I like doing it. I think by working with the tribe, I can make it prosper even without the slave labor the Hendersons used. That's what we were, you know. Even before they sold me in Mexico, I was a slave and didn't even know it. Gonzales paid a very high price for me. At least I think it was a lot of money. It cost Gonzales fifty thousand dollars. Is that a lot of money?"

"It certainly is. Were you worth it?"

"I would have been if I'd been given enough to eat. I've done ranching my entire life. I'm good with all of the animals."

Jon's eyes seemed to sparkle with excitement. "You don't know what I do for a living, but I have a feeling you would do well to follow the path I've taken in life. I'm a veterinarian. I treat all different kinds of animals. If Henderson Ranch is where you want to be, I think I can arrange for a licensed vet to set up a practice there. While you're finishing your education, you can work with whoever is there and learn from someone who has the training and is certified."

Mark could hardly believe what Jon was telling him. With the backing of the tribe where Chris' family were members, along with the training his Uncle Jon was offering him, it made the future of Henderson Ranch sound very exciting.

~ * ~

Phil and Jon stayed at the complex for the remainder of the week. They were pleased to have so much time to get to know their nephew. After the first couple of days, Mark was released from the hospital and returned to his apartment. He also returned to his classes.

The brothers were pleased when they were invited to monitor the classes and see for themselves what Mark was being taught. At first, they were appalled by the simplicity of the classes, but they were told of the advancements Mark made in just a few weeks. Just the thought that a grown man had only minimal education was more than they could begin to comprehend.

During their stay, they met the man Mark credited with his rescue from the ranch in Mexico, Chris Jacobson. Like Mark, Chris' name wasn't his family's name. While he'd been brought up on Henderson Ranch, his fate had been to join one of the skinhead groups that seemed to be perpetually bringing in young militants.

They both thanked Chris profusely for saving Mark's life. As they expected, Chris brushed off their praises, saying it was only right that the boys who he grew up with be given the same opportunity that he'd been offered.

"I do hope you're planning to visit us soon," Jon said to Mark, as they prepared to leave the complex.

"I am. We have a break coming up from schooling soon. I know that Chris will be going back to Nevada to testify against the people who sold him to the militant group. If it would work well for you, I would like to come down to visit and check out your veterinarian practice. I'd also like to meet more of my family. I don't ever want to be alone again."

# Chapter Ten

Mark missed his uncles when they left to return to Texas. He was glad he'd promised to come for a visit when the classes took a break. Since his testimony wouldn't be necessary at the trial for the people who assisted the Hendersons in the selling of the boys who aged out of the program, he would be free to make the trip to Texas and reunite with more of his family. From the little he'd gathered when Henderson took him to Mexico, Mr. Granger was given a cut of the money the ranchers paid for the slaves they purchased. He decided the price was so high because there weren't as many children being sent to the ranch as there had been in the past.

Another thing that came as a surprise was his hunger for an education. Like Chris, he'd mastered the rudiments of an education quickly and was soon tackling the high school courses that were interspersed into his education schedule.

It was hard to see Chris leave for Nevada for the trial for the Grangers, but at the same time, Mark was anxious to take his own trip to Texas to spend time on his Uncle Jon's ranch. He was anxious to be working outdoors with the animals he'd loved all his life.

Both Jon and Phil were at the docking station to meet Mark's hovercraft. As soon as he disembarked, they were at his side.

"You look a hell of a lot better than the last time we saw you," Phil said as he pumped Mark's hand.

"I feel a lot better, too. It's been good not to have to worry about the stress of preparing for the trial for Mr. and Mrs. Granger. I've been taking my studies very seriously. It's been interesting to see how much learning I've been able to achieve in such a short amount of time."

"Have you given any more thought to what you plan to do with the rest of your life?" Jon asked.

"Like I told you, I've been offered a position on the old Henderson Ranch when I'm through with my schooling. I love working with the animals and it seems like a sensible option."

"Phil and I have been looking into that property. It seems that your friend Chris' father's family is doing some investing in it. We've been in contact with them and are ready to invest in it too. I'd like to have you work with me at the clinic while you're here. If veterinary medicine is something you'd be interested in, we'd be willing to set up a clinic on the ranch and bring in some of the best teachers of veterinary medicine to train anyone who would be interested in it as well."

Mark was shocked. His vision of the future was riding the range and managing a prosperous ranch. Never in his wildest dreams had he considered veterinary medicine. The prospect of becoming more than a ranch hand was exciting. It was possible this was something he would be able to do.

~ * ~

Jon was excited to introduce Mark to not only his family but also the staff at his veterinary clinic. As soon as they walked through the door to the clinic, Mark's eyes began to sparkle, giving credence to his assumption this might be something Mark would be good at.

Although the boy's experience had been with cattle and horses, every dog and cat in the clinic seemed to gravitate to him, as though they were pieces of metal being drawn in by a powerful magnet.

"Do you only take care of dogs and cats?" he asked.

Jon smiled at Mark's question. "Hardly. These are only the clinic cases. We take care of all types of farm and wild animals, on our ranch, the neighboring ranches, and some of the wildlife sanctuaries. In other words, we are responsible for the animals who have no way to take care of themselves. I try to keep our treatments reasonable for the families of our patients. I make my money from the ranch."

"Do you think I would be able to do something like this someday?"

"I know so. I've been in contact with Cassion and some of your other instructors at the complex. They all agree, with the way you're progressing, it would be possible for you to continue your education as well as begin your studies in veterinary medicine. Don't make up your mind right now. You'll be here for a week. It should be enough time for you to decide if this is something you might be interested in pursuing."

As the day began, Jon allowed Mark to assist with several of the cases that were brought into the clinic for treatment. Mark's gentle touch and calming voice put both the patients and their human owners at ease.

It didn't take long before Mark was giving patients their baths and doing some of the grooming of strays that well-meaning clients brought in off the streets.

"You're doing well with these strays," Jon complimented him.

"Why shouldn't I? They're like me. They're alone and afraid. I remember when I was taken to Henderson Ranch. I was alone and scared out of my wits. For the next fourteen years I tried my best to be friends with Chris and Peter. We all turned eighteen the same year. The first one to leave the ranch was Chris. Mr. Henderson told me to tell Chris about Patrick Ernst's group and make the suggestion he go there. When Peter turned eighteen, he was there one day and gone the next. I never knew what happened to him. Of course, you know what happened to me. Once I left the ranch, I was alone again and more frightened than ever. I know what it's like to be scared."

Jon wiped his eyes with a tissue. "I promise you, Mark, you will never be alone again. You have a family and we're all determined to make certain your future is bright."

~ * ~

For the first time since the night his mother died, Mark had dreams of the future and the end to his lonely existence.

By the end of the week, he completely understood his uncle's passion for veterinary medicine. Even with this limited experience, he knew this was a calling he wanted to pursue.

When Chris arrived back at the complex, Mark was anxious to reconnect and tell him of the new interest he'd found and of his dream for a future on Henderson Ranch.

They both had classes and took their meals together. It was at supper when Chris finally asked the question that gave Mark an opening. "You look like you're bursting to tell me something. What's on your mind, Buddy?"

"I do," Mark replied, "but it can wait. I want to know what happened when you testified at the trial for the Grangers in Nevada."

"The trial was held in the same courthouse as the one for the Hendersons. I was shocked when I recognized Peter. He'd been liberated from another of the ranches in Mexico after we testified against the Hendersons. We reconnected and since you're planning to manage Henderson Ranch, we talked about it. I know we talked about having the ranch be one for unwanted kids, but we both know those days are coming to an end. We think we can find enough of the kids who were at the ranch with us that we can offer them not only a job on the ranch but also an education."

Mark's mind raced with the implication of what Chris was proposing. "Does that mean you and Peter would be willing to return to the ranch?"

"It does. I do think we would have to change the name of the ranch, though."

Mark nodded his head. "I have a feeling what I have to tell you will add more pieces to the puzzle you're laying out. While I was in Texas, I helped my Uncle Jon in the veterinary clinic. I realized this was something I wanted to do with my life. Uncle Jon suggested we open a teaching facility for guys like us who were denied educations. In addition to getting an education they could work on the ranch. I know you want to work with kids, but how would you feel about being in on the process of helping others like us, while teaching them the things they need to know?"

Chris' smile said more than any words. "I was trying to decide how to bring up the same thing to you. I think the future of the ranch is in our hands and we have to do something special there. After meeting Peter,

I realized we aren't the only ones who need help. Do you think we can get Cassion and some of the people at this complex to help us?"

"I do. The first thing we need to do is come up with a new name for the ranch. I've been giving it a lot of thought. What do you think of the name Resurrection Ranch?"

"I like it."

"Do you think Peter will join us? How has he fared since we left the ranch?"

Chris nodded. "I didn't know him at first. He was thin and I could tell he'd been mistreated over the years. He knew me right away. Anyway, we talked about it and he was the one who suggested trying to find the kids who are still being liberated from the ranches and militant groups around the country. One of the things that was brought out at the trial were the bank accounts of Pops and Ma. They also kept meticulous notes on the names of the kids they took from Henderson to be sold to the various groups and ranches."

"Did you learn what they made from selling you to Ernst?"

Mark could see tears forming in Chris' eyes. "I guess I was a disappointment. Ma got the hundred dollars that Henderson gave me and Pops got five thousand dollars from Ernst. Unfortunately, he had to give half of it to Henderson. They made a lot more money from the guys they sold in Mexico. They were all sold for twenty to twenty-five thousand dollars with Pops and Henderson splitting the profits. Guess Henderson was getting desperate when he sold you. He wanted to keep all the money for himself."

"Do you know how we can contact Peter?"

"I have a contact for him at one of the Alien complexes in Mexico. Cassion and I talked about transferring him here, so he can work with the two of us in bringing Resurrection Ranch to reality. Unfortunately, we came to the conclusion he needed the assistance he was getting at the complex in Mexico."

Mark liked the idea and could hardly wait to contact his family in Texas about what he'd just learned. If they could all work together this could become something bigger than any of them ever envisioned.

~ * ~

Later that afternoon, Mark waited for Kara to finish her shift at the hospital. He'd missed her more than he thought possible while he was in Texas.

After sharing a private dinner in her apartment, he told her everything that happened while he was in Texas. It surprised him to see tears welling in her violet eyes.

"Why are you crying?"

"I don't want you to leave here. I missed you more than I could tell you. If you're going back to the ranch in Nevada, what will happen to me?"

"You didn't let me finish. I want to ask Dr. Gratan for permission to make you my wife. I want to set up a medical facility on the ranch in addition to the veterinary clinic. With the number of men we'll need to run the ranch, it would be foolish not to have medical treatment for them. With you as my wife, we would make a good team to bring Resurrection Ranch into being."

"Resurrection Ranch?" she questioned.

"That's the name Chris and I came up with over lunch today."

"I like it, but that means Chris will be leaving here as well. Will Melian be going with him?"

Mark nodded. "I have a feeling he will be asking her to become his wife in the very near future. He loves her as much as I love you. I think the four of us will make a good team. While you and I manage the medical needs of both the humans and animals, they will be overseeing the teaching facility. There are many young men like us who need an education and we hope to be able to provide it as well as a job to any of them who want to join us. In the future, it might all change, but for now, that's the plan."

Kara grasped his hand tightly. "In that case, I don't know why you have to consult Dr. Gratan. My answer is yes, yes, yes, a thousand times yes."

"I was hoping that would be your answer, but since Dr. Gratan is your legal guardian here at the complex, I think it would be the proper thing to do. I know it's proper to give you a ring, but for now that's going to have to wait. I will have to tap into some of the funds that were set aside for my mother and now belong to me, from her family. Once I do, we can choose the proper ring for you."

Without saying more, Kara sat aside her plate and moved closer to Mark on the couch. She put her arms around his neck and hugged him tightly, before kissing him tenderly.

"I'm certain all of this has been orchestrated by the One God. We were meant to meet. I was so disappointed when my parents thought coming to Earth from the far side of the moon was the best thing that could happen to me. I was terrified. Once I got here, I fell in love with the beauty of Earth. It wasn't until you arrived that I knew my future was always meant to be here, with you."

"You know it won't happen for a while. I have a lot of schooling to do before I'm ready to start making plans for the ranch. According to Cassion and the other teachers, I could be completely up to speed by the end of the school session. It's hard to believe, but I've already tested out of several of the courses. I need to concentrate on mathematics and science to prepare for a career as a veterinarian. We will have a lot of time to plan to make everything perfect for the two of us."

# Chapter Eleven

Mark was relieved to have the tests he'd taken at the end of what his instructors called the school term over and done with. He was leaving the classroom when he saw Cassion waiting for him.

"I've been waiting for you to complete your exams," Cassion greeted him. "I've received word from the prosecuting attorney in Arizona. Your father and grandfather are going to be going to trial within the next month. The prosecution has said they want you to testify against them. Do you think you're up to that?"

Mark swallowed hard as he remembered the effects the trial for the Hendersons had on him. "You know I want to see them punished for what they did to my mother, but I worry about seeing either of them again. I honestly don't remember much about my father. It wasn't until I talked to Jason Culver, in Nevada, that I knew my grandfather was anyone other than the bad man. I'd like to talk to my uncles about this."

Cassion nodded. "I thought that would be something you'd want to do. I contacted both of them earlier this afternoon and they will be contacting you on your communicator this evening. I'm certain they will both be ready to testify at the trials. I will also be going with you. I do have a law degree and will be more than happy to be with you to look out for your interests."

Mark was grateful to Cassion. He'd become a mentor and trusted friend. To have him by his side at the upcoming trials would be comforting to say the very least.

~ * ~

Mark waited patiently in his apartment for the communication to come in from his uncles. The first to appear on the screen was Phil. He was soon joined by Jon.

"We had a call from Cassion this afternoon. Are you sure you're up to testifying at the trial for your father and grandfather?" Phil asked.

"I have to be. What they did to my mother is something that should never go unpunished. I realize my father was in prison for beating my mother, but I'm told he is being charged with kidnapping her. I hope it's not too late to prosecute him for that crime."

"I've checked with our attorney," Jon said. "He informed me that because your mother was a minor, and it was apparent he abused her both physically and sexually, there is no statute of limitations. He then took her across state lines, which is also against the law."

"That's a relief. I talked to Cassion earlier today and he has agreed to accompany me to both trials."

"He told us the same thing," Phil said. "Since we both run our own businesses, we will be able to be at both trials. I remember Jon telling me about how you were alone and afraid for most of your life. He promised you'd never be alone or afraid again and we both agree we need to be with you at the trial in Phoenix. I only wish our parents were still here to be there as well. I'm certain they, along with your mother, will be there in spirit to see justice done after all these years."

~ * ~

Things moved so quickly it made Mark's head spin. By the end of the next week, Mark and Cassion were on their way to Phoenix. Rather than staying at a hotel, they were taken to a complex like the one in Denver. The apartment they were assigned was a two-bedroom complete with a kitchen. Even though neither of them was inclined to do any cooking, Mark found it to be an interesting addition to the apartment. Seeing it, he decided something he wanted to learn was how to cook delicious meals like the ones his mother used to prepare.

Once they were settled, they met Jon and Phil with their families for dinner in one of the TexMex restaurants located within walking distance of the complex.

As soon as Mark tasted the entrée that his uncles insisted he should order, he was transported back to when he was a child sitting in his mother's kitchen. Unable to control his emotions, he found tears rolling down his cheeks.

"Is something wrong with your food?" Phil asked.

Mark shook his head. "It reminds me of my mother. When they took me away from the apartment we shared, I longed to eat the meals she prepared for me. I haven't tasted anything like this in far too long."

He quickly looked toward Cassion. "I don't mean that the food at the complex isn't good but…"

"I completely understand," Cassion said. "It's not like what your mother used to prepare. Although the chefs at the complex do a good job, I still miss the meals I ate at the base on the dark side of the moon. I guess we all have memories of what was normal in our childhood and usually isn't duplicated once we become adults."

~ * ~

They next morning, they were all transported to the courthouse for the beginning of Stephen Cruz's trial for kidnapping, abuse and taking a minor across state lines.

Mark had no idea what to expect. Would he have feelings toward his father or would the contempt that raged in his mind for both his father and grandfather take over completely?

The man who entered the room held no resemblance to Mark and he wondered if he was truly Stephen Cruz.

Across the aisle from where Mark and the others were seated, a woman was crying. When the man entered the room, she called out, "Stephen, I love you. I know you're not guilty of what they're charging you with."

"Who is she?" Mark whispered to Cassion.

"She's your father's wife. The two kids sitting next to her are your half-brother and sister."

Mark could feel his stomach churn. He hadn't thought that after what his father did to his mother he would remarry and have other children. Did they even know about him? He doubted it.

The prosecutor gave his opening statement, detailing how Stephen kidnapped Constance Montenegro from her loving family, abusing her and leaving her in the custody of his father when he was incarcerated for beating her.

Mark wished he could see the expression on his father's face, but of course that was impossible. The man sat with his back to the gallery along with the woman who would have been his stepmother if he hadn't been sent to Henderson Ranch, and her two children, his siblings.

When the prosecutor finished, the defense attorney made his opening statement, saying Constance Montenegro left her home willingly to be with him and he'd been railroaded when he was sent to prison for beating her. They'd engaged in an argument and she'd blown everything out of proportion.

Phillipe Montenegro was the first person to take the stand.

"How do you know the defendant, Mr. Montenegro?" the prosecutor asked.

"We were in the same class in high school. I thought we were good friends, until he met my sister. He filled her head with a lot of nonsense about how they were in love. She wanted to quit school, but our father wouldn't allow it. The next night she and Stephen went on a date, but Connie never came home."

"By Connie, do you mean Constance Montenegro?"

"Yes sir. At home we called her Connie. She was only sixteen and until the day he died, our father cursed the name of Stephen Cruz. He was positive Stephen kidnapped her and took her away. It wasn't until recently we learned what actually happened to our sister."

"How did you learn that?"

"We were watching the proceedings for the trial for the people who ran Henderson Ranch. One of the young men who testified was Mark Almanor. Afterward, we contacted a man by the name of Cassion who has mentored Mark and he told us the boy was Connie's son. When we met him and compared DNA, we found he was our long-lost nephew."

"I have no more questions for this witness."

Mark watched as the defense attorney got to his feet. After going through the trial for the Hendersons, he knew the defense attorney would take this opportunity to cross examine Phil.

"Mr. Montenegro, if the boy you met and claim as your nephew is Mark Almanor, how can you possibly be accusing my client of kidnapping your sister. Why aren't you looking for someone by the name of Almanor?"

"My sister was terrified of both your client and his father. After suffering a beating at the hands of Michael Cruz, she moved to Nevada and changed her name to Tessa Almanor. She also changed her son's name from Paco to Marco. Before she could make her way home to her family, she died from internal bleeding."

"That's irrelevant in this proceeding. My client isn't charged with murder."

"He should be. He must have known what his father was capable of doing. My sister was a minor, he stole her away from her family and took her across state lines. That in itself is a crime. I don't know what went on between the two of them. Maybe she thought she loved him and was going willingly. I would give anything to have been able to save her as well as her son."

Stephen suddenly got to his feet. "You lying bastard. Connie and I were in love. We did nothing wrong."

The judge banged his gavel and the defense attorney forced Stephen to sit back down at the defendant's table.

Mark wished, once again, he could see his father's face.

There were no more questions for Phil and he was allowed to leave the stand. Before he took his seat, he gave Mark a thumbs up sign.

Jon was the next to take the stand. His testimony mirrored that of his brother's, almost word for word.

Before Mark was called to the stand, the judge ordered a recess for the midday meal. As they were leaving the courtroom, the woman who had been identified as his father's wife came up to them.

"Why are you doing this to my husband? He's a good man. We

have two children together?"

"May I ask what your name is?" Mark asked.

"I don't see why not, because I'll be testifying for the defense this afternoon. I'm Diana Cruz and these are my children, Stephen Junior and Theresa. I take it you're the little bastard who is trying to say Stephen is your father."

"I am a bastard only because my father never married my mother. He is my father and that makes you my step-mother and your son and daughter my half siblings. It seems like I find more family every time I turn around."

"You are no family to us. Once this fiasco is over, I will thank you to never contact any of us." With that, she turned on her heel and walked in the opposite direction.

"Guess I won't be reuniting with my siblings," Mark quipped.

"She's angry. In the end, I'm certain both Stephen Jr. and Theresa will seek you out," Jon assured him.

Mark had his doubts but kept his comments to himself.

After having their midday meal, they returned to the courtroom for the afternoon of testimony.

Mark was the first person called to the stand.

"Please state your name."

"My given name was Paco Montenegro but I have since changed it legally to Mark Almanor."

"Why have you changed your name?"

"I wasn't even four years old when my mother and I ran away from the bad man. I later learned he was my paternal grandfather, Michael Cruz. My mother had taken a terrible beating and I was also hit. When he left the house, my mother stole money from his safe and we ran away. She told me we couldn't let anyone know who we were. She called me Marco."

"Why are you calling yourself Mark"

"Marco was a frightened child who was all alone in his life. Mark is an adult name."

"What do you remember of your father?"

"Very little. I was barely three when he went away. My mother said he went away because he hurt her."

The defense attorney went on the attack when Mark finished his testimony.

"How do you know my client is your father?" he asked.

"My mother said he was and the bad man said his name when he was hurting my mother."

Mark began to cry and shake uncontrollably as he reverted to his three-year-old self. In his mind he could hear his mother crying in pain and feel the blood running down his lip from where his grandfather hit him. He could hear the old man screaming at him that he was nothing but a sniveling brat and his father, Stephen, would be ashamed of him.

The defense attorney said he had no more questions and Mark was allowed to leave the stand. As soon as he stood, his legs protested. He didn't want to make a scene. Before he could collapse, Cassion, Phil and Jon were at his side, helping him back to his seat.

"Are you all right, young man?" the judge asked.

"He will be," Cassion replied. "Because of this man and his father, Mark has lived through a very traumatic childhood."

"Just who are you?" the judge questioned.

"I am Cassion, from the Council of Intergalactic Affairs. I am a lawyer who is here to represent Mark's interests. He needs to rest. I will take him back to the complex…"

"No," Mark interrupted. "I want to see this through. I'll be fine."

"Then we'll continue," the judge replied.

"The prosecution rests, your honor," the prosecutor proclaimed.

The defense attorney called Diana. "Please state your name."

"My name is Diana Cruz. Stephen Cruz is my husband."

"What do you know of the charges brought against Stephen Cruz?"

"I know these are trumped-up charges. My husband is the gentlest man in the world. He doesn't have a mean bone in his body. He could have never done the things you are accusing him of."

Mark could hardly believe the words coming out of Diana's

mouth. Was it possible going to prison had changed him from the man who beat his mother?

"Do you know anything about the woman he's accused of kidnapping, Constance Montenegro?"

"I'd never heard her name until all of this came about. As for the bastard who says he is Stephen's son, he's a liar. The only children Stephen has are mine, Stephen Junior and Theresa."

The prosecuting attorney had no questions for Diana. Since she was merely a character witness, Cassion assured Mark there was no need in trying to discredit her testimony.

The next witness was Stephen. After stating his name, he took a seat in the witness box.

"Do you know Constance Montenegro?" his attorney asked.

"We dated in high school. When her father wouldn't let us get married, we ran away together. Later she lied to the police and said I beat her. I ended up going to prison because of that bitch."

Mark wanted to jump to his feet and call his father a liar, but Cassion's hand on his leg stopped him.

"Did you have a child with Constance?"

"Yes, I did. His name was Paco, but the bitch wouldn't give him my last name. She was pissed off because I hadn't married her. He could have been anyone's brat. I wasn't around long enough to know if he was mine or not."

"Did you have him DNA chipped?"

"Hell no. That's just a way for the government to keep track of you. She had him at home so that we didn't have to pay a doctor to deliver him or pay to have him chipped."

"Were you aware she was a minor when you took her across state lines?"

"She told me she was eighteen and now I know she lied. When I mentioned that she was three years behind me in school, she said it was because she was stupid and failed three years."

"Do you know what happened to her when you were in prison?"

"My father said he'd take care of her and her brat, even if it wasn't mine."

The prosecutor got to his feet. "Were you or were you not a friend of Phillipe Montenegro?"

"We were in the same class in school, but that doesn't mean we were exactly friends. I knew she was his sister. When she told me she was eighteen, I figured they were probably twins and she got the short end of the stick in the brains department. That didn't matter much to me. She was good in bed, even though I figured she was spreading her legs for several of my friends."

Before anyone could stop him, Mark was on his feet. "Liar," he shouted.

The act brought on the dizziness he'd felt while he was in Nevada. Surer of himself, he refused to give in to the unconsciousness he was certain would follow. There was no way he wanted to show weakness in the presence of his father.

"Do you have a DNA chip, Mr. Cruz?"

"What the hell for?"

"To compare it with Mr. Almanor."

"Yes, I have one, but I'm positive that bastard isn't mine."

The judge looked over at Stephen. "I call for a brief recess so our medical personnel can scan your chip as well as that of Mr. Almanor."

"When did the little bastard get chipped?"

Cassion was on his feet. "If I may, your honor, I would like to answer the defendant's question."

"You may. Please step forward and be sworn in."

Mark watched as Stephen was led back to the defendant's table where medical personnel were ready to read his DNA chip.

"Do you know when Mr. Almanor was chipped?"

"I do. He was orphaned when his mother died and with no identification, he was sent to Henderson Ranch. At the age of eighteen, he aged out of the program and was sold as a slave to a ranch in Mexico. We rescued him when we learned of what was going on at that ranch. By the time we got him to our facility in Denver, we knew nothing of his background. It was at that time his DNA was tested and a chip was implanted. Through that chip we were able to find the brothers of his mother and learn more of what transpired before and after he was born."

Mark quit listening when the medical personnel came to read his chip. It was a painless process, but the way his father acted when he had it done, he was worried about the results. What if Stephen was correct and his mother was sleeping with his friends? Would he actually be a bastard, or after his mother was kidnapped, was she raped? Either way he was ashamed of the man who was now standing trial. He prayed he would be a better man than Stephen Cruz could ever be.

Cassion returned to his seat as the doctor took the stand.

"What were your findings?' the judge asked.

"The scan shows that Mr. Cruz and Mr. Almanor are father and son."

"The court thanks you."

Mark glanced over at Diana. All of the color had drained from her face. To his surprise, Stephen Junior got to his feet.

"I'd like to testify," the young man said.

"You can't," Stephen protested. "You're too young."

"I'd like to hear what this young man has to say," the judge declared. "You may take the stand, son."

Stephen Junior walked past his father, with his head held high.

"Can you state your name and age?"

"My name is Stephen Cruz Junior. I'm fifteen."

"What did you want to tell the court?"

"My mother lied when she was on the stand. She said what my father told her to say. If she told the truth and he got to come home, she was afraid he would beat her again."

"Have you witnessed this abuse?"

"Many times. He's even started beating on me. I was afraid he was going to start hitting my sister. I don't want that to happen."

"Did you know about your half-brother?"

"Not until today, but I'd like to know more about him."

"Thank you for your honesty, son. You can return to your seat."

Mark watched as his sibling came back to the gallery. For a

Sherry Derr-Wille

moment their eyes met and he was certain this wouldn't be the last time their paths would cross.

The judge recalled Diana to the stand. Once there, she recanted her earlier testimony stating that her husband had threatened her with further bodily harm if she told the truth.

Both attorneys made closing arguments and the jury was dismissed. Mark knew it would take a while for a verdict to come in. As he got up to leave the courtroom, Stephen Junior came to his side.

Mark assessed the young man. It was entirely possible that his father had been released from prison shortly after he and his mother ran away from Arizona. If that was the case, he'd probably met Diana around the same time.

"After today, I guess we're brothers. Are you going to be staying in Arizona?"

Mark shook the young man's hand. "No, I'm getting my schooling in Denver and will be moving to Nevada where I've been offered a job as a ranch manager. Once I'm there, I'll be studying to be a veterinarian."

"Will I ever see you again and get to know you?"

"Once I'm on the ranch, it's possible you could come and spend some time there."

"I hope so. I've always wanted a big brother."

"Whatever you do, I think you should clear it with your mother. I don't think she would be too happy with you coming to the ranch. Don't do anything to cause her any more anguish than she's going through."

"I understand. I'm sure Theresa will want to get to know you as well. Of course, we won't do anything without Mother's approval."

Before they could leave the courthouse, Diana came up to them.

"I'm sorry, Mark," she said. "I can't imagine what your life has been like. I lied because Stephen and his father both threatened me. That was foolish. Can you forgive me?"

"I've been learning about the One God and forgiveness. I can forgive you because He has saved me. I hope we can be friends, and I can get to know Stephen Junior and Theresa."

Once they were alone, not only his uncles, but Cassion too

congratulated him, and suggested he should try to get some rest before the jury returned with their verdict.

They were ready to leave the courthouse when the clerk came out to tell them the jury was back with the verdict.

Mark was apprehensive but returned to the courtroom. Across the aisle, Diana and her children looked nervous. Mark couldn't blame them. If the jury did not find Stephen Cruz guilty, there could be repercussions and retaliation against his family.

When asked about the verdict, the foreperson said they were all in agreement. When the judge nodded, the foreperson read the verdict. "On the charge of kidnapping, we find the defendant guilty. On the charge of taking a minor across state lines, we find the defendant guilty."

Diana looked relieved, and Mark could understand why. After his testimony, he worried about his safety if his father wasn't found guilty.

"Stephen Cruz, you have been found guilty of all charges. You are hereby sentenced to life in prison in the state penitentiary, with no chance for parole."

By the time Stephen was led out of the courtroom, he ranted and raved about the unfairness of his sentence.

Mark could still hear him shouting as he was taken out of the room. He was glad this trial was over. He also knew that tomorrow would be the trial for Michael Cruz. It would be just as trying, if not more so, than this one. Rest was what he needed now. He certainly didn't want a repeat of what happened after he was in Nevada for the trial for the Hendersons.

~ * ~

Once they returned to the complex, it was evident Cassion as well as his uncles were concerned. As soon as they entered the apartment Mark was sharing with Cassion, they were met by one of the doctors who serviced the people at the complex.

He knew it wasn't worth protesting about receiving medical attention. His bout with dizziness coupled with the weakness he experienced during the trial alerted him to how fragile his health still remained.

"Is there a problem with my nephew?" Jon asked, once the physician finished his examination.

"When Cassion contacted me, I familiarized myself with his records," he replied.

Turning to Mark, he continued, "You know your body better than anyone, young man. I'm certain Dr. Gratan has advised you of what to look for. Should the dizziness or the weakness return, I suggest you carry something that you can snack on. The abuse on your body has caused you to experience a sudden drop in blood pressure, combined with a drop in blood sugar. I will contact the cook to supply you with snacks you can carry with you. I won't say this is dangerous, but it is good for you to carry something with you to counteract it. For now, I suggest you have a good dinner and get some rest. From what Cassion has told me, tomorrow will be a much more trying day than today has been for you."

# Chapter Twelve

After having a good night's sleep, Mark forced himself to eat the healthy breakfast his uncles had ordered for him at the restaurant of their hotel.

As they ate, Cassion and his uncles discussed the trial that would be starting at nine o'clock that morning.

"Yesterday was bad enough," Phil stated. "Facing Stephen gave me chills. I remember his father and the man frightened me when we were classmates. I was thinking about it last night and remembered how Stephen sometimes had unexplained bruises. They were usually covered by his clothes, but when we had to take showers in gym class, they were evident. When he was asked about them, his story was that he'd fallen. At the time we accepted it, but I think the old man was beating the shit out of him."

"What about his mother?" Mark asked.

"That was something else. It was always just Stephen and his dad. He told us his mother abandoned him when he was very young. He said he didn't remember anything except that her name was Anna. Last night I did a Google search and found she is living in Mesa, not far from where Stephen and Michael moved after they kidnapped Connie."

"Hmmm, that's interesting. Do you think she knows about today's trial?"

"She does now," Phil replied. "I contacted her last night. She said not only did she know about the trial, she'd been contacted by the prosecution as a witness. We'll be meeting her this morning. I asked her why she left and she told me it was for her own safety. As for leaving Stephen behind, she had no other choice. Michael beat her so badly that she almost died. When she told him she was leaving, he told her if she took his son away from him, he would kill her. Also, if she left alone, he'd let her live."

Mark remembered his grandfather making the same threat to his mother. He knew it was the reason she'd stolen the money from the safe and the two of them left while no one else was in the house.

~ * ~

The courtroom was packed when they finally arrived. Mark was pleased to see Diana, Stephen Junior, and Theresa sitting in the gallery. He acknowledged them with a nod of his head. To his surprise, Stephen Junior came to where he was sitting.

"My family wants to get to know you better," Stephen said. "We talked about things last night and my mother has decided to have our last name changed to her maiden name of Alverez. I also made the decision to go by my nickname of Buck. Theresa also wants to be called Terri. We want nothing to do with the man who fathered us."

"You've made a good decision, just as I did when Cassion helped me to have my name changed legally."

"We've been doing some research, especially after what you said about taking over Resurrection Ranch. Mom wants to know if there would be a place for us there? She's a trained teacher as well as a good cook. We want to be included in your project."

Mark was taken by surprise. "I don't know, Buck. All of this is in the planning stage. What about your educations? You and Terri deserve more out of life than living on a cattle ranch."

It was Cassion who joined them. "I couldn't help overhearing your conversation. I have been working behind the scenes, so to say, to get Mark's project off the ground. Since we are planning to have an educational facility on the property, I am certain your mother would be a welcome addition to the staff. From what I've been told, there is a house on the property that is being rehabbed. It might take us a few months, but I'm positive something can be worked out. Mark deserves to have the family he's been denied for his entire life."

The bailiff announced that court was in session and everyone should take their seats, ending their conversation.

Mark's mind was still reeling from what Buck just told him when he saw the object of his nightmares enter the room. It was amazing how much smaller Michael Cruz appeared. When Mark was a child, he thought his grandfather, the monster, was at least seven feet tall and strong as an ox. As an adult, he saw an old man. His once-black hair was now completely white, and it was evident he stood just under six foot tall.

Like the day before, he only saw his grandfather's face for a brief moment before he was seated at the defendant's desk. He found he was much more comfortable staring at the old man's back. If they didn't make eye contact, he wouldn't be intimidated by the bad man of his past.

The prosecutor laid out his case of how Michael Cruz had taken custody of Constance Montenegro and her son when his son Stephen had been sent to prison. Because of his cruelty, Constance was forced to flee his home after he had severely beaten her, causing her untimely death.

The first witness was Jason Culver.

"How did you come to know of Constance Montenegro, Officer Culver?"

"I was on patrol in Elko, Nevada. It was at the end of my shift around four thirty in the morning, when I saw a young boy alone on the sidewalk. He told me his mother wouldn't wake up and he was hungry. When I asked him where he lived, he directed me to an apartment building, not far from where he was standing."

"What did you find in the apartment building?"

"I found an apartment door open. When I went in, the rooms were very neat. As I walked through, I entered a bedroom and found a young woman lying in the bed. I tried to wake her, but her body was cold to the touch. It was evident she was dead and had been for several hours. As we did more investigation, we learned the name on the lease she'd signed for the apartment was Tessa Almanor and she was living there with her son, Marco. That was the name the little boy gave me when I found him on the sidewalk."

"What did you learn was the cause of her death?"

"The medical examiner who did the autopsy told me she died a slow and painful death from a beating she'd taken. He said there were several ruptured internal organs and she slowly bled to death. It was enough to make me sick to my stomach."

"What happened to the child?"

Jason looked directly at Mark before he continued his testimony. "Since he had no family that we could find, he was sent to Henderson Ranch. At the time, I thought it was going to be the perfect place for him. I'd heard how they were funded by the state of Nevada and took in orphans to raise them. It wasn't until recently that the world learned he'd been sent to hell on earth."

"How did you come to equate Tessa Almanor with Constance Montenegro?"

"It wasn't until I read about the trial for the Hendersons. When the trial ended I met Mark Almanor. That was when I remembered a missing person's report I'd received about a month after finding Tessa and Marco. It was put out by Michael Cruz and he was looking for Constance Montenegro and her son Paco. At that time, everything seemed to fall into place. I talked to Mark and he confirmed that his name had been Paco, but his mother told him never to tell it to anyone because the 'bad man' would find them. It didn't take long for me to realize the 'bad man' was Michael Cruz."

As much as the defense attorney tried to shake Jason's story, he could not be swayed to change his testimony.

The next person to take the stand was Anna Manning. Mark looked at the attractive older woman who he knew was his paternal grandmother. She was a small woman, hardly a match for the bad man of Mark's nightmares.

"How do you know Michael Cruz?" the prosecutor asked her.

"We were married for six years. After I gave birth to our son, Stephen, I thought we had the perfect marriage. By the time Stephen was four years old, Michael changed. He started abusing me, mentally, sexually and physically. I told him I was leaving and taking Stephen with me. He told me if I took his son away from him, he would kill me to get him back. He made me promise I would leave my child and never go to the police in order to save my life. Over the years I have often wondered what happened to my former husband and my child. Little did I know they had moved to the Phoenix area, just a few miles from my home in Mesa."

"Did you divorce Michael?"

"I did, but my lawyer could never find him. They were looking for him in Nebraska where we were living at the time of our marriage. I have since met a wonderful man and have an entirely new family and identity. I didn't realize they were living in this area until I was contacted to testify at this trial."

The prosecutor ended his questioning and was replaced by the defense attorney.

"You testified that you abandoned your four-year-old child. Is that correct?"

"I told my husband I wanted to leave with our son, but he wouldn't allow it. I was lucky to have escaped with my life. I prayed my husband had not abused our son in the same way he did me."

"Yes, but you abandoned your son. Doesn't that make you an unfit mother?"

"I was not an unfit mother. I was a young woman in fear of losing her life. The only way I could escape was to leave my child. Had I stayed, Michael would have killed me. Had I taken my son with me, he would have killed me to get his son back. I left to protect myself as well as my son. Without me, I was certain he wouldn't kill our son."

The attorney kept badgering Anna until the prosecutor finally objected to his method of questioning. Once the judge made a decision about the line of questioning, Anna was excused.

Mark could tell the woman who was his grandmother was shaken by her experience. He knew the cold stare from his grandfather frightened her, even though she remained composed.

Finally, it was Mark's turn to take the stand. Cassion told him he would be the star witness for this proceeding.

After he stated his name and his age, he made the mistake of making eye contact with his grandfather.

"How do you know the defendant, Michael Cruz?" the prosecutor asked.

"I never knew his name. What do names mean when you're three years old? I remember he wanted me to call him Grandfather and later Papa. I only thought of him as the bad man."

"Did you ever see your grandfather strike your mother?"

The small child in Mark threatened to return. "More than once."

"Did he ever hit you?"

Mark nodded his head as the words seemed to be stuck in his throat.

"Please Mr. Almanor, you must answer verbally."

He swallowed hard. "Yes, he did. The last time was the night my mother and I ran away from him. He was beating my mother and I yelled at him to leave my mother alone. He turned on me and hit me so hard I flew across the room. When I stood up, blood was running down my lip. I was afraid he was going to kill me."

He answered a few more questions before the defense attorney began his cross examination.

"You tell quite a story, young man. With children's memories, it's hard to tell fact from fiction. You called my client the bad man. Wasn't that like when children are afraid of the boogie man under the bed. Isn't this all a figment of a child's overactive imagination?"

Mark was appalled, but determined to hold his temper in check.

"I've made up nothing. I've relived the life we endured every night in my nightmares. It wasn't until recently that I was able to put a name to the bad man from my past."

"You testified that you and your mother left your grandfather's house. Can you tell me about how your mother stole money from your grandfather?"

"It was the night he beat my mother for the last time and made my nose bleed. My mother told me she took money from Grandfather's safe so we could run away and start a new life."

"Was that when she changed your name?"

"Yes, it was. She told me I should never tell anyone my real name was Paco and from now on I would be Marco. I thought it was a strange game, but I was happy that we would have to be hurt by the bad man any longer."

"Do you realize your mother was a criminal?"

"My mother was a good woman. She only took the money so we could get away from him." Mark got to his feet and pointed his finger directly at his grandfather.

The courtroom erupted in gasps of amazement, causing the judge to bang his gavel on his desk, ordering everyone to be quiet.

Once again Mark could feel the anxiety he'd felt yesterday at the trial for his father. As much as he wanted to eat one of the snacks the doctor suggested he carry with him he knew eating one would be inappropriate while on the witness stand in court. Unfortunately, he'd left them on the bench where he'd been sitting when he got up to testify. Willing himself not to succumb to the urge to give in to unconsciousness, he took a deep breath and tried to calm himself.

"Are you okay to continue, Mr. Almanor?" the judge asked.

Mark opened his mouth to reply, but no words would come out. Instead, a warm blackness encompassed him and he pitched forward.

~ * ~

Jon could see his nephew was in trouble. Being a court proceeding, he knew it would be inappropriate for him to go to the witness stand to take Mark something to eat. He could only watch in horror as Mark pitched forward in a dead faint.

Getting to his feet, he was immediately at Mark's side. Behind him the courtroom was abuzz at the turn of events. Amid the chaos, the judge was pounding his gavel and calling for order.

With Phil at his side, they worked together to lift Mark's dead weight that was hanging over the witness box to the floor.

It came as no surprise when he heard sirens. Someone must have called for assistance. Behind him, he heard Cassion explaining Mark's condition to the paramedics. To Jon's relief, Mark began to come around.

"Here," he said, "eat this."

He handed Mark a soft protein bar. Almost like magic, the dull look in his eyes disappeared and the color began to return to his cheeks.

"We need to check you over, sir," the lead paramedic said. "We've been apprised of your condition, but we would like to make certain your vitals are returning to normal."

Jon backed off as Mark nodded his head in approval.

~ * ~

Mark's worst fears came to fruition when he lost consciousness. As much as he hated being the center of attention, suddenly the attention of everyone in the courtroom was centered on him.

After the paramedics took his vitals and were satisfied that he was in no immediate danger, he allowed Jon and Phil to help him to his feet.

Once he was again seated, he was surprised when Cassion was called to the stand to testify.

Cassion stated his name and Mark waited patiently to hear what his mentor was going to be asked.

"Cassion, you have testified that you are one of the Aliens from the Denver Complex. What is your connection to this case?"

Mark listened as Cassion detailed how Chris had come to the complex and been rescued from the militant group. With his rescue, Cassion said, it became a mission of his to find other survivors of Henderson Ranch.

"When Mr. Almanor was brought to your complex, what was his condition?"

"He was suffering from malnutrition and dehydration. What happened here is a side effect of what he was suffering from. He was treated last night after the trial for his father yesterday. He has been abused for his entire life and is only now coming to grips with the ramifications of what has been done to him."

Mark wanted to stand up and shout his life wasn't what mattered here. It was what his grandfather did to his mother that mattered, but he refrained. The truth had to be told no matter what the consequences in his life.

He hadn't realized that Cassion was done testifying until he heard the judge announce they were recessing for lunch.

Still feeling unsteady, he got to his feet and left the courtroom with his uncles. He didn't know why Cassion was lingering behind them, but at the moment it didn't matter. He'd finished his testimony and although he needed to be there for the reminder of the trial, he felt a rush of relief come over him.

Off to one side, he saw Diane and her family engaged in conversation with Anna. He wondered if he should make the effort to connect with the older woman, this stranger who it seemed was his paternal grandmother.

"I feel a bit overwhelmed with all of this family," Mark confessed.

"You've had a lot to digest these past couple of days," Phil said. "For now, you need to care for yourself. When and if you're ready to connect with Anna, I know how to contact her."

There was no time for Mark to agree or disagree with his uncle, as the older woman had left the family he met yesterday and made her way to his side.

"I realize this must be overwhelming for you," Anna said. "I just want to tell you how proud you make me. I've regretted leaving your father with my ex-husband all my life, but I knew taking him away would have been a death sentence for me."

Mark felt suddenly sorry for the woman standing in front of him. "If he'd killed either you or my father, I would not be here. I have a feeling the One God has a purpose for me and it doesn't include never being born. I want to get to know you and I'm certain we will be getting together in the future. For now, though, I need to take care of myself and make a workable plan for the future."

"I can understand that. All I ask is that you don't forget me." With that, she backed away and returned to where Diana and her family were standing.

"You handled that well," Cassion said, coming to his side. "You were right to give yourself time to replenish your energy. When the time is right you will be able to reconnect with your grandmother."

~ * ~

If Mark thought he'd seen the last of his father, he was sadly mistaken. The first witness for the defense was Stephen Cruz. He was brought into the courtroom wearing an orange jumpsuit and his hands were electronically shackled.

After he was sworn in, he took the witness stand.

"How do you know the defendant?" the defense attorney asked.

"He's my dad."

"What about Constance Montenegro? How do you know her?"

"She lied about her age and encouraged me to run away with her. We lived together and had a son, Paco, but she kept hedging about getting married. One night we were having an argument and she called the cops on me. The bitch was very convincing and I got sent away to prison."

"What became of Constance and Paco?"

"My father took her into his house, out of the goodness of his heart. Neither of us were happy about her not giving our son my last name. Even so, he looked after her and the brat until the night she took money out of his safe and disappeared. We didn't know if they were dead or alive, but since we were never married, I found love with another woman and built a real family. By the time I was released from prison, they'd disappeared. I said good riddance."

"What about the accusations that your father beat not only her but also your son?"

"She was a conniving little bitch, I'm certain she told people a very convincing story. I have no doubts that she's dead, but it was probably because she was using drugs and overdosed. I wouldn't put anything past her. The people who are trying to pin a murder that might or might not have happened almost sixteen years ago on my father are lying just like she did."

The smile on the face of the defense attorney said he thought the jury would believe every word that came out of Stephen's mouth.

The prosecuting attorney got to his feet and walked across the room to stand in front of the witness box. "I have the autopsy report for Constance Montenegro. It states that she died of internal injuries as well as bleeding from those injuries caused by a beating. There were no drugs in her system. What do you have to say about that?"

"Cops are cops, no matter where they are. They've had it in for my family for years. I'm certain they were more than happy to have the report doctored to suit their purposes."

"Until recently, no one knew that Constance Montenegro and Tessa Almanor were one and the same. That being the case, why would anyone have a reason to doctor the report for Tessa Almanor?"

The expression on Stephen's face was one of shock. Everything he'd testified to was being destroyed by the evidence in the autopsy report.

When Stephen was excused, an officer came and led him away. It was possible he was being held in a facility in Phoenix before he and hopefully his father would be transferred to the state prison.

Mark was surprised when Michael didn't take the stand in his own defense. When he questioned Cassion about it, he was told it would, more than likely, do more harm to his case than he would do good.

With no further witnesses, the attorneys gave their closing arguments and the jury left to come to their decision about guilt or innocence.

Like the jury the day before, the verdict was reached within an hour of the start of deliberations. The results were guilty of murder in the second degree.

"Michael Cruz, you have been found guilty of murder in the second degree," the judge said. "I wish we could have proved that the murder of Constance Montenegro was premeditated so I could sentence you to death. Of course, we know that is no longer an option. Since that is not the case, I sentence you to life imprisonment at the state penitentiary with no chance for parole."

Before Michael could be shackled and taken out of the courtroom, he turned to face Mark. "This is your fault, you little bastard. If your mother hadn't been such a lying little bitch who stole money from me, none of this would have ever happened. It's too bad I didn't kill her and you on the night she ran away and stole my money. I hope you burn in hell for what you've done to me."

His grandfather's words shocked Mark, but he refused to stoop to the old man's level. It would have been easy to lash out against him and repeat the vile words he'd spoken. With what he'd learned since being brought to the complex, he realized giving hate for hate was nonproductive. In spite of his upbringing, he knew he'd grown into being a responsible adult who could learn to forgive.

~ * ~

Mark was surprised when they returned to the complex and found an invitation to meet Anna, as well as Diane and her family, at a restaurant not far from the complex. The invitation included Cassion, Jon and Phil, as well as Mark.

Although Mark was apprehensive, Cassion insisted it would be the perfect way to end such a trying day.

The restaurant Anna chose was one of the most elegant restaurants in Phoenix. Mark prayed his manners would not be an embarrassment to him. He'd gone from eating the slop served at the ranch in Nevada, as well as the one in Mexico, to the nourishing food at the complex. Although he'd eaten at restaurants while away from the complex to testify at the trials, he'd never been anywhere this fancy in his entire life.

"Whether you like it or not," Anna said, once they were seated at the table and their orders were taken, "you are my family. Mark, you, Buck and Terri are my grandchildren. If things had been different, Diane, you would have been my daughter-in-law. I am not without means. In other words, my late husband left me very well off. Unfortunately, my children from my second marriage no longer live in the area. My son, David, is an architect in Dallas and my daughter, Cindy, is married to a doctor who works in Peru. That said, I want to get to know all of you better. I would be honored if you would allow me to invest some of the money in Resurrection Ranch."

Mark was at a loss for words. Two days ago, he had no idea these people even existed and now he was coming to grips with the thought of them being his family. Earlier he'd agreed to Diane, Buck and Terri coming to live and work on the ranch. Now this woman, his grandmother, wanted to invest in his future. It was completely overwhelming.

It was Jon who replied to the offer. "I think we can all work together on this. My brother and I are both investing in Resurrection Ranch. Cassion has offered his help and several people from the Denver Complex are interested in coming there to work as well. What you need to know is there are several young men, like Mark and his friend, Chris, who have been deprived of an education and a family because of the Hendersons and the way they ran the ranch for far too many years. To begin with, the ranch will be catering to educating them and giving them a secure future."

"I've done my homework. When I first read about my ex-husband being charged with murder, I didn't think it had anything to do with me. I was interested in what I was reading about my son, as well as the two families he had. I thought about the fact I had grandchildren I might never know. If I hadn't gotten the communication from the prosecuting attorney, I would have found a way to connect with all of you at a later date.

"For you, Mark, it breaks my heart to know how you were raised and the horrors you've survived. I want to make a difference in your life.

"That brings me to Buck and Terri. I have a feeling the two of you suffered more than any of us will ever know at the hands of your father. It pains me to think my son followed in the footsteps of his father. They are both cruel men and I pray that you two becoming involved with Resurrection Ranch will break the chain of brutality that has ruled this family for far too long."

"I didn't give you enough credit, Anna," Jon said. "It hasn't been that long since Phil and I were the ones asking Mark to accept us as family. At the time we doubted his connection to us, but the DNA proved he was definitely our nephew. Yesterday, your son also doubted Mark, but again the DNA brought about a revelation I'm sure he didn't want to accept. You are more accepting than any of us."

Mark agreed with his uncle. This woman who was his grandmother didn't need any tests to prove who he was. She was offering him unconditional love and support.

"All my life, I've wished I had a family," he finally said. "I don't remember much about my father, but I do remember my mother. I've always thought she was the only family I would ever have and she'd been taken away from me. Now suddenly I have uncles, a grandmother, a step-mother as well as a half-brother and sister. You'll all have to bear with me, because this is something completely unknown to me. I don't know what to do with family."

Anna got up and came to where Mark was sitting. "You might not know what to do with us, but we know what to do with you. Let us into your world and let us love you."

Mark could no longer contain the tears that were threatening to fall. He cried for his mother who wouldn't wake up, for the childhood that was stolen from him, and for the future he thought was over when he was sold as a slave.

# Chapter Thirteen

Returning to the complex was bittersweet for Mark. As much as he longed to be with Kara, he knew he would have like to have stayed longer in Phoenix and get better acquainted with the family he'd just found.

When the hovercraft docked, he and Cassion were met by both Kara and Hodia. While he understood his feelings for Kara, he was surprised to see what could only be called love between Cassion and Hodia.

"We watched both of the trials on our communicators," Kara said. "I was so worried when you passed out at your grandfather's trial. I won't even go into how you looked at the end of the trial for your father."

"We were staying at the Phoenix complex and the doctor there did a complete examination. He said my problem was a combination of a drop in blood pressure and low blood sugar. If I'd had one of the snacks that he suggested I carry at Grandfather's trial, I wouldn't have lost consciousness."

"Still, Dr. Gratan wants to have me bring you directly to the hospital for a complete physical."

"I'll do what you say, but it isn't necessary. Cassion made certain I got plenty of rest before we returned. I've also been eating better than I have in my entire life. I want to hear about you and what you did while I was gone. One of the young technicians from the dark side of the moon didn't try to steal you away from me, did they?"

"You know better than that. I told you how much I love you. I agreed to become your wife. I'm looking forward to helping you and Chris rebuild Resurrection Ranch."

Mark pulled her into a tight embrace and kissed her lovingly. "That's something else I need to talk to you about."

"We'll have plenty of time for that. For now, if I don't get you to the hospital, Dr. Gratan will send out the security force to come and find us."

From behind him, Mark could hear Cassion chuckle. "I think this little lady has your number. It's always best to do what your woman wants."

Mark turned back to see Cassion and Hodia holding hands. "Do you always do what your woman wants?"

"You bet he does," Hodia replied with a sly wink.

~ * ~

Dr. Gratan was pleased when he finished his examination and told Mark there was no need to hospitalize him. When Mark told him what the doctor in Phoenix concluded regarding his condition, Dr. Gratan completely agreed.

"He was lucky to get to see you right after you had one of those episodes. For now, I see no reason not to allow you to go back to your apartment. I'm certain Kara will be pleased with my decision as well."

Mark nodded. When he left the office, he found Kara waiting for him in the lounge area.

"I got a clean bill of health. No hospitalization. I can go back to my apartment."

"I'm relieved. Since you have something to tell me about Resurrection Ranch, perhaps we can go there now and relax a bit before it's time for the evening meal to be served."

Together they made their way to the elevators. Mark decided it would be good for the two of them to be alone so he could put everything that transpired while he was in Phoenix into perspective.

"Now what did you want to tell me?" she said, once they were seated in the living room of Mark's apartment."

"Since you watched the trials, you know my father had another family. I wasn't certain I wanted anything to do with them. After the verdict was in, they approached me. My father's wife is filing for divorce and changing her last name back to her maiden name of Alverez. She's also changing her first name to Diane. His kids, my half-brother and sister, are also changing their names. Rather than being Stephen Cruz Junior and Theresa Cruz they will be known as Buck and Terri Alverez. Anyway, they want to make a complete break and move from Arizona to Resurrection Ranch. I questioned why they wanted to do that. Their mother said she is a trained teacher and would like to be part of the educational program. She's also willing to do the cooking, until we can engage a full-time chef. Buck and Terri are also wanting a fresh start. I know I'll have to talk to Chris about it, but I do see where they would all be a good addition to the staff of the ranch."

"That is so exciting. I was worried that Melian and I would be the only women on the ranch. I can hardly wait to meet all of them."

"There is more. I did meet my paternal grandmother. She has made a new life for herself in Arizona and is not without financial means. She wants to invest in the ranch. She is discussing the possibility with my uncles. I can't believe how all of the pieces to the puzzle are coming together."

"I was excited about what our futures will look like before and I'm even more excited now. Since it's almost time to go to the dining hall, perhaps we can meet up with Chris and Melian and eat together. We all have a lot to talk about, especially since his family is also backing the ranch."

~ * ~

The dining hall was relatively quiet when they arrived. They didn't have to wait long for Chris and Melian to arrive.

"We watched the trials on our communicators, Buddy," Chris said, when they joined Mark and Kara. "I was worried about you, but you handled yourself well. How hard was it facing your father and grandfather?"

"I won't kid you. It was hard. Of course, I couldn't remember what my father looked like since he went to prison when I was very young. The cross-examination was rough and I guess I didn't do too well, because I ended up being examined by the doctor at the Phoenix complex.

"Grandfather's trial was much harder, because I had to look the old man in the eye. I was better prepared though, or at least I thought I was. Blacking out wasn't what I planned to do, but it happened."

"It certainly did happen. I watched you slump over. I thought for sure they'd done you in. I thank the One God you're okay."

"It's going to take a lot more than passing out to get rid of me. Enough about that. We need to talk about Resurrection Ranch."

Chris raised an eyebrow. "What more is there to talk about? My mother's family has purchased the ranch, or at least the tribe has. That said, my father's brother is making a financial contribution. I've come to the decision that between Melian and myself we're going to set up the educational program. You'll be managing the day-to-day operation of the ranch and Kara will be working at the medical facility. What more is there to talk about?"

Mark repeated the story he told Kara earlier about the members of his family that he'd met at the trials and how they wanted to be involved with Resurrection Ranch.

"I can't believe they want to relocate to the middle of nowhere from Phoenix," Chris exclaimed.

"I couldn't either, but after the trial they wanted nothing to do with the name of Stephen Cruz. Why else would they go to the expense of changing their names and moving away from the familiar to embrace the unknown? I was concerned about Buck and Terri, but they both assured me they knew exactly what they were doing. I can't imagine them returning to their former life when everyone knows about their father's trial."

"I agree," Melian said. "I had a friend, before I came here, whose father committed a terrible crime and was sent to the penal colony. She was so ashamed she took her own life. It was shortly after that when my parents decided it would be best if I came here with my Aunt Zora. The whole thing bothered me and I was worried my friends would think I was bad because of what she did. Coming here, where no one knew me, was the best thing I ever did."

Chris put his arm around her shoulders for a side hug. "I know it was the best thing that happened to me."

"We're off the subject," Mark interjected. "The other person I met was my paternal grandmother. After leaving my grandfather many years earlier, she built a new life for herself. She's a very wealthy widow and she wants to invest in the ranch as well. I'm sure by now my Uncle Phil has contacted your Uncle Chester so together they can work out the best way to spend the money they now have at their disposal."

"You are right. We have both been blessed with being able to reconnect with our families and having it be a good thing. Do you think we can help the others do the same thing?"

"That's a hard question to ask. We have been able to find Peter, but what about the others. How many of them do you think are still alive? I mean, Juan was at the Gonzales ranch before I got there. I was told he'd been beaten to death. It was a serious warning for me to follow the rules or the same thing could easily happen to me."

Mark was glad when they decided to table their discussion until they finished their meal. While they ate, the girls talked about the plans they were making for their roles at the ranch.

"I've been in contact with Peter ever since the trial for the Grangers," Chris said, as they enjoyed their dessert. "He's excited about coming to the ranch. While you'd make a good manager, he'll be an excellent foreman. Hopefully, we can find enough of the kids to bring back for rehabilitation."

"I think I'm privy to some information you two aren't," Kara said. "While you were at the trials, I was talking to Dr. Gratan and he expressed an interest of transferring out there. I mean, you will be needing a medical facility. As a nurse I can do just so much."

"You aren't the only one who is doing research," Melian said. "I talked to Aunt Zora and she said Hodia and Cassion are also talking about giving up their positions here. Chris and Mark have made quite an impression on both of them."

Mark was overwhelmed by the information he'd just received. He knew that with the amount of people who were planning to come to live and work on the ranch, there was a lot of refurbishing that needed to be done.

"I've been drawing up some plans," Chris commented. "Would the two of you like to join Melian and me at my apartment to look over them?"

"Plans?" Mark inquired.

"While you were gone, Uncle George was able to make a trip down to the ranch. You know, the tribe bought it sight unseen. He and several of his friends decided he should send me some pictures of the buildings. They are in a lot worse shape than I remember them being. The drawings of the plans are for the repairs that have to be made. Since most of us are good at not only ranching but also carpentry, I think we can do a lot of the work ourselves. I know Peter was excited when I told him about the rehabilitation project."

Mark's interest was piqued enough that he was anxious to see, not only the plans, but also the pictures Chris' family sent.

~ * ~

The table in Chris' living room was littered with photographs he'd been able to print from his communicator, as well as several drawings.

Mark was impressed. He had no idea about his friend's artistic talents. "The dormitory doesn't look much different than it did when we were there. In other words, it's going to need a lot of work to make it livable. As I recall, the wind would blow through the cracks and the roof leaked like a sieve."

He shuddered at the mental picture the photographs brought to his mind. Seeing the pictures brought back the terrible memories of growing up, never knowing when you were going to be punished for some supposed infraction of the rules.

"Are you all right?" Chris asked.

"I will be. Seeing these pictures makes me wonder if I will ever be comfortable going back there."

"I know what you mean. They affected me the same way. The more I look at them the more excited I get. I know with everyone who is planning to help us we can transform it into exactly what the name implies."

Mark shifted his attention from the disturbing photographs to the pencil drawings. Chris' renderings of what Resurrection Ranch could look like were awe-inspiring. He wondered if all the backers of the project would be as excited about seeing them as he was.

# Chapter Fourteen

Mark's dreams were filled with the time he spent at Henderson Ranch. In them, he relived the horrors of everyday life as he'd known it for the majority of his life.

The bedside clock read two AM when his communicator woke him up. He was drenched in sweat as he looked at the screen, surprised to see the face of the night doctor from the hospital unit.

"Are you all right, Mark?" the young woman asked.

"I-I was dreaming."

"Your numbers are off the charts. I'm sending a nurse up to your apartment with something for you to eat. He will monitor your numbers until we're satisfied that you're out of danger."

Mark nodded his agreement.

Once the connection was closed, he sat back, marveling at the modern technology that allowed his vitals to be transmitted to the hospital even when he was in his apartment. He was still thinking about what just happened, when he heard the automated voice signaling someone was requesting entrance to his apartment.

As soon as the door slid open, he recognized Terrin, one of the night nurses from the hospital. During the time he'd been a patient there, they'd become good friends.

"Dr. Jamison sent me up with some foods to regulate your blood sugars," Terrin greeted him. "She was very concerned when she saw the rapid drop in your numbers."

Mark picked up the glass of orange juice and enjoyed the sweet nectar as it slid down his throat.

"How did she know?" Mark asked.

"When you returned from Phoenix, Dr. Gratan added a chip to your communicator to monitor your vitals and send abnormal readings back to the hospital's main computer. In that way you can be monitored night and day. Dr. Jamison and Dr. Gratan both agree that your condition is something called hypoglycemia. Over the next few days, they will be coming up with a treatment plan so that you don't have such dramatic drops in your numbers."

Mark was confused. Throughout his life, he'd never known of any illnesses. Even if he had been sick, the Hendersons never took any of the kids to the doctors. If they were sick, they still worked. No one ever worried about if a kid got sick and died.

"Is this life-threatening?" he finally asked, once he'd eaten some of the food on the tray Terrin brought.

"No, but it has to be managed. We are blessed to have such advanced technologies that we can detect problems before they need drastic measures. Tomorrow, arrangements will be made for your apartment to be equipped with a kitchenette so you will have access to prescribed snacks. You'll also be educated on how you can keep track of your numbers for yourself and how to recognize the signs of what is happening to your body."

They talked until the sun was cresting the eastern horizon. Although Mark knew he should have tried to get more sleep, he appreciated the company Terrin provided, as well as the information he had to impart.

From his communicator, the alarm signaled it was time for him to begin his day and for Terrin to end his shift.

"I hope you don't get into trouble for spending so much time with me," Mark said, as his friend stood to leave.

Terrin smiled and shook his head no. "Dr. Jamison anticipated you wouldn't be able to get back to sleep and instructed me to stay with you. She knew I would be able to begin the education you need about your condition. That doesn't mean you can forgo the education Dr. Gratan has planned for you, though. While you're in the shower, I'll program information on how to contact me into your communicator. If you ever need me to assist you or if you just want to talk, you can call on me anytime."

Mark nodded his agreement and made his way to the shower in order to become refreshed to begin his day.

~ * ~

Mark's classes for the day consisted of history, mathematics, and science. By the end of the day, he was amazed by the amount of information he'd been provided. As usual, he felt as though his mind was a sponge, eager to soak up any and all of the things that were being taught to him.

Even though it was still early afternoon, when his classes finished, he made his way across the compound to the hospital unit. When he arrived, Kara was waiting for him.

"I heard you had a bad night," she greeted him.

"Nightmares," he replied, hoping she wouldn't probe further.

"Your chart says it's more than nightmares. Dr. Gratan and Dr. Jamison are waiting for you in the conference room. They want to start your education on how to manage your hypoglycemia."

"Will you be with me?"

A bit of color flushed Kara's cheeks. "Dr. Gratan feels it would be best if I accompany you, considering we will be married sometime after we go to Resurrection Ranch."

Although Mark didn't know much about romance or what transpired between a man and a woman, he allowed his body to dictate his next move. Without thinking about whether anyone else might see, he pulled Kara into a tight embrace and kissed her tenderly.

"How did I ever get so lucky to be brought here and find someone like you to love?"

"It has to be the doing of the One God. Of course, Chris did play a part. We can't forget that without him wanting to find you, none of this would have happened. Now, enough of this. The doctors are waiting for us."

Mark agreed. For now, he wanted to learn how he should begin living his life knowing how to care for himself in case of another drop in blood sugar.

~ * ~

By the time Mark and Kara met Chris and Melian for the evening meal, Mark felt as though his head was about to explode. What Terrin told him in the early hours of the morning was but a minute portion of the information the doctors imparted to him. Being told he needed to eat several small meals each day came as a surprise. Never, since he'd been with his mother, had he been told to eat several times a day. Growing up he'd become used to two scant meals each day and when he was sold to the ranch in Mexico, he'd learned to get along on one meal of watery soup.

"What did the doctors have to tell you?" Chris inquired.

Mark told him about the diagnosis and his need to eat several times a day.

"That doesn't sound too bad to me. I could take a prescription like that one," Chris teased. "So how are you planning to be able to eat during the night when you can't come to the dining hall?"

"I can answer that," Kara commented. "While you and Mark were attending your classes, changes were being made to Mark's apartment. He will have a small refrigeration unit installed as well as a cabinet where snacks can be stored. Both of them will be restocked daily so that the doctors can keep track of what he's eating or not eating. With this condition, what he eats is very important. I met with the doctors this morning and we all agreed it was imperative that the diet is followed consistently."

Mark was pleased to have Kara explain the things he was just now beginning to understand. It felt as though getting used to eating smaller meals throughout the day was going to be difficult. Even looking at the meal on his tray, he wondered how he would manage to eat all of the food that would be allotted to him.

"Are you sure this is something I should be eating?" he asked, indicating the meal sitting in front of him.

"Positive. Your dietary restrictions have been sent to the kitchen and the portions are exactly what you should be eating. I'm anxious for you to see the changes that have been set up in your apartment. If I'm not mistaken, there will be detailed instructions as to when to eat and what you should eat at each of the small meals. I only wish we were already married so I could be with you to make certain you do what you're told."

Mark looked at Kara lovingly. She was so important to him, he wanted her to be his wife and not have to wait. Still, he knew waiting was necessary. He knew her parents would want to be at the ceremony as well as the new family he'd recently found.

# Chapter Fifteen

It had been three weeks since Mark returned to the complex from Phoenix. In that time, he'd adjusted well to his new lifestyle. Eating more small meals every day kept his health on an even keel.

Together with Chris, he'd been making more and more plans for the ranch where they would be living and working within the next few months.

He was just returning to his apartment when he received a notification of an incoming message on his communicator. Before responding, he entered his apartment and made himself comfortable on the couch.

Accessing the message, he was shocked to see the face of his father fill the screen.

"Hello," he said, even though he knew he had nothing to say to the man on the other side of the screen.

"Hello, Mark, or should I say Paco?" Stephen greeted him.

"My name is Mark. I have no idea why you are communicating with me."

"You're my son. I have a right…"

"You have no rights where I'm concerned," Mark interrupted. "You kidnapped my mother, got her pregnant, beat her unmercifully and sent her to live with the monster who finally took her life."

"Your mother and I were both young when we ran away to be together. She was being mistreated at home and…"

"And nothing. Thank goodness my mother was strong enough to call the authorities and have you arrested for beating her. If she hadn't, it would have been you who killed her rather than Grandfather. As far as I'm concerned you are both monsters. The only thing I want from you is an explanation as to why you are communicating with me."

"I want to ask for your forgiveness. I've been meeting with the chaplain here and am learning about the One God. I know what I did to you and your mother was wrong, but that's in the past. I need to put my life in order and make amends."

"That's interesting. I've been learning about the One God as well and for some reason I don't believe a word of what you are saying to me. Because of you I grew up alone with no one to love me. The only person who did love me when I was small was Mother, but your father took her away from me. Maybe he didn't physically kill her the night she died, but he beat her so badly he caused her death. Forgive you? Why should I? Will it lessen the time you spend locked away from the world? I doubt it. I will pray on it, but don't expect miracles."

Mark closed the connection and made his way to the kitchenette. The exchange with the father he neither knew nor wanted to know, left him drained. Sweat was beading on his forehead and his hands shook. He knew what he should be doing, but he couldn't make his hands and mind coordinate to choose a snack.

"Mark, Mark, are you all right?"

He recognized Terrin's voice. "I-I don't know what to do."

The words no more than left his mouth than he could feel the blackness of unconsciousness overcome him.

Kara was almost ready to leave the hospital when Terrin came to her side.

"Mark's in trouble. His sugar has plummeted. Can you get us into his apartment? I have a feeling he's lost consciousness."

Kara grabbed her bag and accompanied Terrin to the elevators that took them to Mark's apartment. Weeks earlier, she'd been given clearance to enter Mark's apartment without him with her. She never thought there would be a need for it, but tonight she realized it was a necessity.

When the elevator stopped on his floor, she hurried to his door. Pressing her palm against the pad, she held her breath as the door slid open. Inside the apartment, she saw Mark lying on the floor between the kitchenette and the living room.

With Terrin's help, she was able to get him moved to the couch, where Terrin was able to administer a shot of glucose. It took only moments for the color to return to Mark's face and his eyes to open.

"What happened?" Kara asked as she took his pulse.

"I had a communication from my father. I knew I needed to get something to eat, but when I got to the kitchenette, I couldn't remember what to do. The last thing I remember is Terrin calling my name through the communicator."

Kara nodded. She'd studied the different reactions to various diseases when she went to nursing school. At the time she doubted she would ever need the knowledge, but she was a good student. Until tonight she'd never been called upon to put the information into practice. It was amazing how quickly everything she'd learned in school came back to her.

Mark tried to get up, but she insisted he lie back and rest. While she checked his vitals, Terrin prepared an appropriate snack to help raise Mark's blood sugar.

"I think we should contact Cassion," she said, once she was assured Mark's condition had stabilized.

"Why?" he questioned.

"There should never have been a communication between your father and you while he's incarcerated. There will need to be an investigation into how he was able to contact you. What did he want?"

"He said he'd found the One God and he wanted me to forgive him. I told him I would have to think about it. I don't think he meant any harm, but it was unnerving. I never thought I would have to see him face to face again."

Kara was fuming. "There is absolutely no reason for that man to ever make contact with you. We definitely have to alert Cassion about this. I think the courts made a big mistake by sending that man to a state prison. Apparently, their security isn't as strict as that in the penal colonies."

~ * ~

Mark had no idea when Cassion had been contacted. One minute he was telling Kara about the conversation with his father and the next he was repeating the same story to Cassion.

"This is not acceptable," Cassion declared. "Heads will roll. What kind of security do they have at that institution? There had to be some breech for that man to be able to have access to a communicator. We will be sending a delegation down there first thing in the morning to have this investigated. Thank goodness your communicator has the ability to record the conversation. As soon as I have it downloaded, we will begin the investigation."

Mark had no idea that the communication he had from his father had been an infraction of the rules governing the state prison where the man was being held.

"What will happen to him?" he finally asked.

Cassion thought for a moment. "I'm more familiar with the procedures at the penal colonies. I can guarantee you allowing prisoners unauthorized use of communicators is punishable by solitary confinement for many days if not weeks or months. It's not only for the prisoner but for the personnel who allowed it to happen. Punishment for things like this are carried out without mercy."

The thought of someone who had been taken in by his father's silver tongue and persuasive personality being given the same punishment as the man who deceived him bothered Mark.

~ * ~

Within a week, Cassion brought news of what happened when his representatives went to the prison where Stephen Cruz was being housed.

"I was shocked with what the people I sent to the prison found out. You weren't the only one he contacted that night. He also called Diane and harassed her. The authorities have found out who gave him the communicator. It was one of the female guards. She was not only fired, but arrested and charged with a felony. As for your father, they are petitioning the courts to send him to a more secure facility. From what I can ascertain they are contemplating sending him to the penal colony under the ice cap of Antarctica."

Mark took a deep breath. It was a lot to take in, but whatever happened to his father was of the man's own doing.

"What about my grandfather? Is he also being transferred to another facility?"

"From what I've been told, he's being a model prisoner. Considering his age, sending him to a more secure facility would be an instant death sentence. As long as he follows the rules of the prison, he will do well where he is."

# Chapter Sixteen

Anna Manning sat in the waiting room of her lawyer's office. Ever since the trial for her former husband, she'd been contemplating the offer she'd made to Mark after the trial. She'd done her research diligently. After talking to the Montenegro brothers as well as George Little Horse, and Chester Jennings, she realized the extent of their involvement in the rebuilding of Resurrection Ranch.

"Anna, it's good to see you," Judith Nolan greeted her. "I was surprised when I saw your name on my client list for this morning. I hope nothing is wrong."

"Not wrong, really, only different."

"Are you talking about the Cruz trial? I saw on the news that you were a witness for the prosecution. Did you know those horrible men?"

Anna lowered her head. "I was married to Michael Cruz and Stephen was my son."

"Was?"

Anna could hear the question of horror in Judith's voice, just as she'd heard it when she told her children of the plans she was making for the future. It seemed as though everyone knew of the Cruz family, although the only one she'd confided in about her previous life was her late husband.

"My first husband was Michael Cruz, and Stephen is our son. He was very young when Michael began abusing me. Those were terrible times. I threatened Michael with a divorce. He told me I could leave his home but without our son. He told me if I took Stephen with me, he would kill me to get him back. What mother, in her right mind, would put the life of her child in danger? When I did file for divorce, Michael and Stephen were nowhere to be found. I was granted the divorce and heard nothing more about either of them until I read about the trial and was called upon to testify."

The expression on Judith's face was one of total disbelief. "That means you have grandchildren you never thought you'd have."

"I most certainly do. Mark is a man now. In reality, his growth was stunted when his mother died and he was little more than a toddler. He has big plans for his future. His friend Chris' family has purchased the ranch where the two of them grew up. They have plans to rebuild the ranch as a rehabilitation facility for the young men who also grew up there and were abused. I want to invest in this venture."

Judith sat quietly for a moment. "You have two other grandchildren, or so I've been told, as well as your two children. What about them?"

Anna smiled. "I've talked to both of my kids. They're excited about having two nephews and a niece to add to our family. They both said that they would rather I spent my money on the grandchildren as they are both secure in their professions and lives. My son, David, is as excited about the plans for Resurrection Ranch as I am. Once I run the idea past Mark, he would like to be involved as well. With his background in architecture, he would be a great asset to the project. My daughter, Cindy, is also excited about the future of our family.

"That leaves Buck and Terri. They're both teenagers and this business of the crimes committed by their father is hard on them. They are both willing to change their names and move out to Resurrection Ranch. The extra bonus is that their mother, Diane, is a trained teacher. The young men who will be coming to the ranch are like Mark and Chris. They were all denied an education when they were residents of Henderson Ranch.

"From what I've learned, Resurrection Ranch will be a working cattle ranch, as well as have a superior education program and a top-of-the-line medical facility. They have the backing of not only Mark and Chris' families, but the aliens from the Denver Complex are also heavily involved. We both know how things get done when the aliens are involved."

"I should know," Judith replied. "I'm directly descended from the original aliens who came to this area. I know all the history of how we came here and the strides we have helped mankind make over the last seventy-five years. Knowing they are involved in this project means things will be happening at warp speed. So, what exactly is it you want to do?"

Anna smiled at Judith's revelation. She'd suspected Judith's family heritage in the past but never mentioned it before this.

"I want to donate to Resurrection Ranch, not just for Mark but for Buck and Terri as well. These kids need to know something good from the paternal side of their family. From what I've learned, Buck and Terri, as well as their mother, have been abused by their father. I know my ex-husband has a financial fortune. The state has asked Diane to administer his businesses as well as his accounts. Diane is planning to liquidate everything and I totally agree with her decision. She wants to put the profits aside for the children's education, but I want to also invest in Resurrection Ranch. I'd like your input on this matter. I'm planning to use some of my own money to finance Resurrection Ranch. Of course, the money from Michael's assets will be more than enough to finance Buck and Terri's education. What better use for it than to help out Mark as well."

"I applaud your intentions. You've been deprived of your son and your grandchildren for far too long. I'd be honored to handle your end of this for you. We have a good financial planner involved with our law firm. I'd like to call him in on this meeting. I can set up the legal aspects of what you're proposing while he will be able to handle the financial end of things."

~ * ~

Three hours later, Anna left Judith's office. Everything had been set into motion. From here on she would not have to worry about her monetary contribution to Resurrection Ranch and anything Diane was willing to invest from Michael's holdings. She knew she could trust Judith as well as all the members of her firm to handle distribution of the money.

After stopping for a light lunch, she made her way to Diane's home. Being spring break, she knew her grandchildren would both be at home rather than in school.

It was Buck who answered the door. "Grandma Anna, I'm surprised to see you here. Won't you come in?"

As much as she wanted to embrace her grandson, she refrained. Such a show of affection would have to wait until a closer bond was established.

"Thank you. I'm hoping your mother and Terri are both here. We have a lot to discuss."

Buck led her into Diane's sunny kitchen, where her daughter-in-law and granddaughter were in the process of making cookies.

"Anna, it's good to see you," Diane greeted her. "Have you had lunch?"

"Yes, dear, I have. I didn't come here to impose on you. I merely want to let you know of the arrangements I made this morning with my lawyer."

"Arrangements?" Diane questioned. "What kind of arrangements?"

After Diane poured her a cup of coffee and put a plate of warm cookies on the table, Anna began.

"I'm certain I made it abundantly clear, at the trial, that I'm not without financial means. Since then, I've been considering your offer to have me help administer Michael's assets. I spent the morning with my lawyer and have set up a fund to financially assist Resurrection Ranch. I've also put money in trust for Buck and Terri to pay for their education. Since the three of you are in the process of changing your names and breaking all ties with Stephen, I'd like to have you move in with me in Mesa until the renovations at Resurrection Ranch have been completed. It would give you a new start without the stigma of being Stephen's children hanging over your heads. Never think, for a moment, that I would ever invade your privacy. I have a large home, with a mother-in-law suite. It was originally built on to the house for my mother-in-law. After she died, it's remained empty. Since I learned of your existence, I've been thinking of moving into it so you can have the house."

"I don't know what to say," Diane said. "This is your home, are you willing to share it?"

"I'm more than willing. Before all this happened, I was toying with selling the house and moving into something smaller. At the time, I considered moving to Dallas, where my son is, and split my time between there and visiting my daughter in Peru. Now that I have family closer to home, I'm rethinking my options. I have a feeling I'm far too old to be an asset to Resurrection Ranch in any way other than financially. I do want to find something closer to the ranch in Nevada, but nothing is carved in stone as my father used to say. Anything could happen between now and when you are able to relocate. It will be a wait and see proposition."

Diane looked at her children. "What do the two of you think about Anna's idea?"

Anna was pleased to see the smiles on her grandchildren's faces.

"Like I've been saying all along," Buck said, "I want to get as far away from Phoenix as possible. Since the trials, I've had some terrible communications from the people I once thought were friends. Someone even told me I should kill myself before I became an abuser like my father and grandfather. I want to go somewhere that I can be me and not live in our father's shadow."

She was surprised when Terri voiced the same opinion. She hadn't thought about the situation Stephen put his children in. Learning of their father's past and living through his abusive nature had to have been hard on both of them.

"How soon do you think you can join me in Mesa?" she finally asked.

"I've already checked into our finances and started the process of liquidating both Stephen's assets and Michael's. Thank goodness I had a good lawyer. I'd been contemplating divorce for several months and together we learned Stephen put my name on everything so he wouldn't have to pay taxes on them. I've been working for several years and agreed I would pay all of the property taxes, not knowing everything was in my name anyway. He owned the house outright and was more than happy for me to pay the taxes. Little did I know his name wasn't on any of our possessions. For my children, I think we could be ready to move within the next week. I can put our furnishings in storage until we are ready to move to Nevada. I appreciate you giving us a chance to begin our new lives earlier than we ever thought we could."

Anna could see the load of frustration and doubt lift from her grandchildren's shoulders. Today was a new beginning not only for them but also for her.

~ * ~

It took very little time for Anna to move her personal belongings from the main house to the mother-in-law suite. In anticipation of her newly found family accepting her offer, she'd aired out the apartment and done some painting in order to freshen up the living quarters that she would be using once they moved from Phoenix to Mesa.

She was also ready to put the house on the market as soon as the arrangements were made for the move to Resurrection Ranch, and the new lives they all anticipated they would enjoy.

On the day Diane and the children were due to move in, Anna made one last check of the main house. This had been her home for the past thirty-five years. Here was where she and her husband raised their children and enjoyed being empty nesters. His death, due to a tragic accident, had devastated her.

For months she'd lived in the house, reliving the past and wishing she could change the unchangeable situation she found herself in.

As she walked through the living room, she recalled the communicator call from the prosecuting attorney asking her to testify against her ex-husband. At that very moment, the past she'd buried deeply within her memory came flooding to her present.

The last thing she'd anticipated was learning she had a daughter-in-law and three grandchildren. From that moment forward, she knew she had a renewed energy and reason to live. She was ready and willing to help shape their lives.

Earlier, she'd put the picture of her late husband in the bedroom that would now become hers. At the time, she spoke aloud to him, as she had every day since his passing. She'd poured her heart out to him and disclosed her plans for the future.

To her surprise, she'd heard his voice within the confines of her mind.

*"I wish we had known about your family before my death. I would have loved to have known your grandchildren and had the chance to spoil them. I'm pleased to think our home will be filled with young voices once again. I'm even happier to know you're thinking of selling this place and playing an important part in their lives. David and Cindy have been communicating with me in their nightly prayers and they are so excited about what your future holds, I know you're making the right decisions."*

The words she heard her husband transmitting to her were the confirmation she needed. She'd always thought she was psychic, but the fact her husband had been able to communicate with her from beyond the grave only gave her further proof of her earlier suspicions.

The home security program alerted her to the fact a hovercraft was preparing to arrive at her docking station. Excitedly, she hurried to the front door to greet Diane, Buck and Terri.

"I'm so glad you were able to find my place," she said, as soon as they were walking up to the front door.

"It wasn't hard," Buck boasted. "Your directions were great and the GPS was able to follow them to a tee. Mom even let me pilot since I got my learner's permit last week."

While Anna held the door open, her family made their way into the house. She could sense their amazement at the show of wealth the house represented. She certainly hadn't looked at it that way in several years. This was her home. It was the house she and her late husband purchased together and furnished to suit their tastes over the years.

"I still don't know how you are able to move out of here to say nothing of letting virtual strangers move in," Diane said.

"I think Mark said it best. He told me Paco was a frightened toddler, Marco was an abused child and Mark is his identity for the future.

This house is the life I lived with my second husband, it's where we raised our children, and enjoyed our time of being empty nesters. When he died, this house was empty and lonely. I've been ready to sell it and move on for several months now. I decided to move to Dallas to be closer to my son, but he has encouraged me to devote my life to your family as well as Mark. You've all given me a new reason to live. Let me embrace you and find the new direction that the One God has chosen for me."

She was surprised when both Buck and Terri got to their feet and came to where she was standing to embrace her. This was what she'd missed the most. When her children grew up and went out on their own, her husband filled the void in her life. Since his passing, she put on an optimistic face and didn't let anyone know how hollow she now felt.

After basking in the love her grandchildren were demonstrating for a few moments, she motioned toward the kitchen.

"I didn't know what you liked to eat, so I took a chance when I ordered food from the market this morning."

She busied herself, filling the counter on the top of the island with all of the fixings for sandwiches, and several salads she'd ordered from the deli.

Buck was the first in line. She knew he would be as ravenous as David had been at that age. As she remembered, teenage boys seemed to have hollow legs when it came to food.

"You should let your grandmother go first," Diane admonished.

"Don't be ridiculous. Growing boys need nourishment. It does my heart good to see him eat. Especially knowing the life Mark grew up living. I can't imagine children not being given enough food to help them grow."

By the time lunch was finished, Anna knew about the grandchildren's activities and goals. Terri was interested in dance and was an exceptional artist, even though she knew she would need other skills in life, she loved doing the activities that gave her satisfaction. Her long-term goals were to own a dance studio and teach young children. Anna knew she could be instrumental in helping her granddaughter in any way possible.

As for Buck, he wanted to be a veterinarian. It amazed her as to how much like Mark Buck truly was. While Mark loved ranching, she knew he'd come to the decision he would never be more than the ranch manager, due to the delicate condition of his health. After talking to his Uncle Jon, she realized that veterinary medicine might be a perfect fit for him as well as for Resurrection Ranch.

# Chapter Seventeen

Mark finished the last of his classes prior to summer vacation. He would have a week to prepare to leave for Nevada to begin the work on the renovations needed at the ranch. The idea of spending his summer working on the renovations and assessing the animals on the ranch was exciting and frightening at the same time. He'd said nothing to anyone at the complex, but for the past several weeks, his sleep time had been dominated by visions of the ranch where he grew up. Would he be able to return and turn it into the money-making operation Chris' family envisioned it would be when they purchased it?

It would still be a while before it was time for the evening meal, so he went out to the garden beside the church where he could have private time to think about the future that was looming ahead of him.

Everything was exciting when he was talking with Chris, as well as Peter, but once he was alone, concerns became the most foremost things in his mind. Only yesterday, he'd learned there were a total of nine former residents of Henderson Ranch who had been found.

They were willing to return for the summer to help with, not only the rebuilding of the facilities, but also to decide if they wanted to become permanent residents in order to receive their educations and decide about their futures.

He was deep in thought when his communicator indicated an incoming message. Glancing down, he saw Cassion's face on the screen.

"Hello," he answered.

"Hello, Mark, where are you?"

"I'm in the garden by the church. I needed some thinking time."

"I completely understand that, but you have a visitor. Can you come to the conference room?"

"Of course. Give me a few minutes and I'll be there."

Mark closed the communication and picked up the backpack he'd placed on the bench when he first arrived. It was heavy with the computer and notebooks he'd used in his classes. He wished he'd taken it to his apartment earlier, but it was too late now. Someone was waiting for him in the conference room.

~ * ~

David Manning waited nervously to meet with his nephew. When he first learned about Mark, he decided he wouldn't make contact until he could formulate his plans for how he could be of help in the rebuilding of Resurrection Ranch. With his expertise in architecture, he decided he wanted to be involved in the project.

It had taken him several weeks to arrange for his clients to be taken care of so he could spend the entire summer at the ranch. Just last week his mother had moved to an apartment in the nearest town and Diane, along with her kids, were ready to move as soon as there were accommodations ready for them.

He'd contacted the tribe who purchased the ranch and they had sent him copies of the pictures of the existing buildings. To say he was appalled was a gross understatement. They all needed so much work it would be for the best if they were bulldozed and replaced with new structures. He hoped Mark would agree with his assessment of the situation.

The only building worth saving was the main house. From what he could ascertain, it had been well maintained over the years. It was also possible it was quite modern on the inside. The comparison between that and the other buildings was enough to make him sick.

He'd talked to his fiancée about his plans for the summer and she was ready and willing to go to Nevada with him to help in any way she could. Being a teacher, she had the entire summer off and was already at the apartment she'd rented in town. Although he wished she would be able to live with him, he knew it wouldn't happen until they were married. Therefore, he'd rented an apartment in the same building as his fiancée and his mother. All in all, it would be an interesting and exciting summer.

Behind him, he sensed, rather than heard, the opening of a sliding door. In anticipation of meeting his nephew, he got to his feet.

Although he'd watched the entire trial for Michael Cruz, he was surprised to see how much Mark resembled his grandmother. He could see touches of Michael in the young man, as well as those of Jon Montenegro, whom he'd met about a month ago. He had no trouble in accepting Mark as a blood relation.

Cassion was also on his feet, and was quick to introduce him to his nephew.

"Mark, this is your uncle, David Manning."

The young man stepped forward and held out his hand in greeting.

"Grandmother Anna told me about you. I didn't know if we'd ever get the chance to meet."

"I've been putting a lot of plans in motion. Last month I met with your Uncle Jon and he had some good ideas for expansion of the ranch in the future. For now, we need to make all of the buildings habitable. In most cases that could mean tearing down what's there and starting from scratch. Since I'm an architect, I've made arrangements to spend the summer helping you."

From the look on Mark's face, he knew his nephew was pleased with his offer.

"We won't be leaving for about a week. My friend Chris is being married on Saturday. I'm certain he will want to spend the time with his family and that of his wife before he returns to the ranch. I, on the other hand, will be free to leave the day after the wedding."

"Mom told me you have a special person in your life, will she be joining you?"

"Kara and I are planning to be married in the fall, giving me the opportunity to have a place for the two of us to stay. It will also give her family time to make arrangements to come here from the dark side of the moon."

"I completely understand your position. My fiancée has already moved to Nevada for the summer. I tried to talk her into moving in with me but she said no way without being married. From the amount of work that we have to do this summer, maybe it's a good thing we aren't married yet. I did take the liberty to have some trailers brought to the property so there are accommodations available for the workers. I'm told in addition to you, Kara, Chris and his wife, and your friend, Peter, there will be about nine others who will be coming to help with the rebuilding."

"Yes, that's about right. I was thinking we could use the old dormitory, but trailers sound like a good idea."

"They are, especially since we'll be bulldozing down the dormitory. I was sent pictures of the buildings, and there's no amount of rehab that can save them. The time and money it would take would be better spent in building new facilities from the ground up."

"That's another thing, the money. I have no idea where we will come up with the needed finances."

David smiled at his nephew's concerns. It was evident he had no idea of the amount of money that was available for the rehab for the ranch and its buildings. The money pledged from Michael Cruz's holding alone would be enough to fund the entire project for the summer.

~ * ~

Mark was immediately comfortable with his Uncle David. He reminded him of Grandmother Anna. It was surprising how each of the family members he'd met since he arrived at the complex fit so perfectly in his life. It was as though all of these people had been part of his life since day one.

Before they went down to the dining hall for the evening meal, Mark went back to his apartment and Cassion took David to the room that was arranged for his stay.

Once Mark left his backpack in his apartment, he stepped into the hallway to be met by Chris.

"I had a visitor today," Mark greeted his friend.

"Interesting, the way things are going around here, I have a feeling it's another relative. I know that's who all of my visitors are."

"You are right. I told you about Grandmother Anna Manning and how she's investing in the ranch."

Chris nodded.

"Well, today her son arrived. That's makes him my uncle. He's an architect and is going to be with us for the summer at the ranch to help with the work."

"I must say the One God works in mysterious ways. I've been going over all the plans for the ranch and I wonder how we'll ever get all the work done. I've also been thinking about that drafty old dormitory."

Mark laughed. "When I met with Uncle David, he addressed some of those issues. He wants to bulldoze the dormitory and build a new structure."

Chris' expression turned to one of concern. "Where will we house everyone, if not in the dormitory?"

"He's got that covered, too. He's bringing in trailers for everyone. Since the house is in fairly good shape, I think it would be perfect for Diane, Buck and Terri to move in."

He watched Chris' expression. He knew Chris and Melian were planning to live in the big house, but with the trailer, it made more sense for his family to move in there.

"I think that's a good plan. With all the work we need to do this summer, neither Melian or I will have the time to keep up that big house. Besides, it's a lot more room than the two of us will need. The way I see it, this is going to be one hell of an adventure."

~ * ~

By the time they arrived at the dining hall, Melian, Kara, Cassion, Hodia and David were waiting for them.

"This is so exciting," Kara exclaimed. "I know I should have waited for you to introduce us, but Cassion already did the honors. I am so pleased to know you are finding more family members. He's been showing us the drawings he has for, not only the dormitory, but also for the apartments, and the educational and medical facilities."

134

Mark was surprised and a little annoyed that David shared his drawing with the others before he got to see them. Rather than show his annoyance, he looked at the drawings that were set on the table where they would be eating their evening meal.

He looked to Chris to see how he would react to the plans David brought with him. To his surprise, they mirrored Chris' plans quite well. The only exception was the drawings for the dormitory. In Chris' drawing, the dormitory was repaired and looked much like it did when they were kids. The new building was modern in appearance and allowed private accommodations for up to twenty individuals.

In addition to the dormitory, there was a multi-story apartment building. It would easily accommodate the amount of people who were planning to move to the ranch to make it into a premier facility.

"There is one other drawing I'd like for you to see," David said. "When I met with Jon Montenegro last month, we discussed the possibility of building a veterinary practice as well as a school on the property. He said you were interested into getting into veterinarian medicine and your half-brother, Buck, has expressed a similar interest. I can see where, not only the school, but also the practice would make a lot of sense. You'll be running several thousand head of cattle and from the research we've done, there is no other veterinarian in the area to care not only for your animals but also those of the surrounding ranches."

Mark could hardly believe what he was hearing. He'd talked to Jon about attending veterinary school in the future. The plans he was seeing now were more than he ever expected.

"How do you think we will be able to get all of the work completed this summer?" he finally asked.

David laughed. "I know all about the carpentry you were taught while you were at Henderson Ranch, but with all of the advances in the industry, buildings can be erected much faster. What the two of you don't know is the amount of funds you have at your disposal for this project.

"I understand your uncle is investing, Chris. That along with the fact the tribe of your mother's people purchased the land means there is more than enough money to get started.

"Now that your family is involved, Mark, there are even more funds available. Your mother's side of the family have put a large donation for the building of the ranch. Since my mother is also involved, she made a donation. Added to that there is the money from the liquidation of your grandfather's assets. They have been turned over to my mother and Diane. In turn, they earmarked a portion of them for the restoration of Resurrection Ranch. Therefore, you shouldn't have to worry about where the funds will be coming from."

Now Mark and Chris were both smiling. They had no idea what to expect when David said he was getting involved. The plans put forth far exceeded what they were planning for the ranch that had been their home as children and was now their future as adults.

# Chapter Eighteen

The following week seemed to fly. After several meetings with David, both Mark and Chris were more than pleased with all of the plans that had been made.

It was hard to say good-bye to David, but Mark understood the necessity of it. His uncle was anxious to get started on the renovations at the ranch. He wanted to make certain the trailers had been delivered and were ready for the number of people who would be arriving within the next week.

With David's departure, the complex buzzed with the activity associated with Chris and Melian's wedding. His family arrived from Chicago at about the same time as Melian's family arrived from under the ice cap of Antarctica.

Meeting Chris and Melian's family showed Mark the diversity of the two cultures. Having met Chris' Native American family at the trial for the Hendersons made him aware of how different this wedding was going to be.

Chris told him of the plans for a service by the pastor at the church at the complex as well as those performed by the priest who was coming with Melian's family. The unknown factor was the service planned by the Native American side of Chris' family.

Contemplating the ceremony that would be taking place on Saturday, he thought about what his wedding to Kara would entail. He wished they would have made plans to be joined together at the same time as Chris and Melian. Unfortunately, planning their ceremony would be more complex, since Kara's family would have to come from the dark side of the moon. Travel from there took longer to arrange than that of Melian's family. They would be well situated at the ranch before there would be another shuttle between the moon and Earth. Shuttles were only run on a quarterly basis and reservations had to be made months in advance. The first reservation they could make was for the fall run.

"You're deep in thought," Kara said as she joined him in the dining hall.

"I was wishing we were the ones who were going to be getting married this weekend."

"You know I do as well, but I do want my family there. Besides, the thought of being married on the ranch is intriguing. I'm packed for the trip as well as Dr. Gratan. We're both excited about opening first the clinic and later the hospital. We both talked to your Uncle David and laid out our plans for both facilities. His plans look great."

Mark nodded. He, too, had seen the plans and could easily envision the finished product. "I never asked, are any other medical personnel going to be going with us?"

Kara smiled. "Are you talking about Terrin?"

Mark nodded.

"He was the first one who asked to join us. The reason my family couldn't get here earlier is because of the number of medical school graduates who are excited to immigrate to Earth. There are more positions here than there are at home. I know I was pleased to be able to come here when I graduated. There just wasn't a position for me there. From what I hear, Dr. Jamison will be taking over Dr. Gratan's position here and there will be a young doctor coming from the moon to take her place."

"I had no idea. I guess I wasn't paying enough attention."

"You've had a lot on your plate. From what I'm told, you've surpassed all the expectations of your instructors. You've been able to test out of many of your classes and excelled in all of the others. What you should have learned as a child, you were able to accomplish in the first months you were here at the complex. The work you've been doing is at the high school level. By the time the educational facility is completed you should be ready to begin your studies to become a veterinarian. From what I hear, your brother is also planning to take on the same studies. Can you imagine the possibilities of the two of you running a veterinary practice? The future is so exciting, I can hardly wait to see how it all plays out."

Mark completely agreed with Kara. He had come to realize he would never work as a cowboy on the ranch due to his health. Working as the ranch manager was what he anticipated, but the thought of becoming a vet was something he knew he would enjoy. He could only hope someone among the other young men who would be interested in the management position.

~ * ~

The morning of Chris' wedding dawned bright and clear. Dressed in the suits that had been supplied for them, they waited in the room behind the altar at the church for the ceremony to begin.

It was easy to see Chris was nervous about what the day would entail. Although they'd been briefed about what would happen at the two traditional ceremonies, the plans made by Chris' Native American family were a well-guarded secret.

Both George Little Horse and Chester Jennings waited in the room with them, possibly in the hopes of soothing Chris' wedding nerves.

From beyond the door, they could hear the music begin, signaling it was time for the uncles to take their seats with their wives in the congregation.

"Relax, Buddy," Mark commented. "It's almost time to get this show on the road. Before you know it, your bachelor days will be over and the two of you will be committed to each other for life."

Before Chris could answer, the pastor came to tell them it was time to leave the small room for the ceremony to begin.

Mark followed Chris to take his place at the altar. Once they stood side by side, the music changed once again. From the back of the church, Kara started her walk down the aisle. On cue, Mark stepped forward to take her arm and lead her to her position on the opposite side of the altar.

As he took her arm, he, once again, wished this was their wedding. Even knowing their ceremony would be taking place within the next four months, he was impatient. He thought of something he once heard about wanting immediate gratification.

Once again, the music changed, and Melian appeared at the back of the church, with her father beside her. The sheer height of the aliens always stunned him. It gave them almost a regal look. Melian's father could easily be a king escorting his princess daughter toward her soon-to-be husband and her future.

By the time they reached the altar, Chris stepped forward and allowed Melian's father to place her hand into his.

Never having witnessed a wedding before, Mark watched and listened intently to everything that was going on. He knew his wedding would be nothing like this, but it was best if he was prepared for what lay ahead for him.

He had no questions when it came to the wedding night, because his instructors had been very careful to make certain he fully understood the differences between men and women. He knew what happened and that women were creatures to be cherished rather than to be considered whores as Mr. Henderson always told them.

It seemed as though the ceremony hardly started before it ended. As they exited the church, Mark was surprised to see two fires burning in the garden. He wondered if this had something to do with the Native American ceremony.

This time, Mark and Kara could watch as a part of the gathered congregation. They had to wait for several minutes until Chris and Melian reappeared. He was surprised to see they had changed from their wedding finery to traditional Native American regalia. Melian wore a white doeskin dress with beautiful red and blue beading. Chris' outfit was of the same beautifully tanned leather. He wore a fringed shirt as well as leather pants. It had the same bead work as the pattern on Melian's dress. To complete both outfits, they wore moccasins like the ones depicted in his studies of Native American history.

Mark watched in awe as his friends made their way to the two fires that were burning. Before them stood a shaman in authentic regalia. His appearance took Mark's imagination from the twenty-second century to a time before the white man came to take the land from these noble people.

After the old man gave his blessing, he announced that the fire to the north was Chris' past and the fire to the south was Melian's past. His next command was for the couple to push their individual fires into the larger pile of dry wood between the two, officially joining them for life.

The entire service impressed Mark greatly. He wished he could claim Native American blood in order to have a similar ceremony when he and Kara were joined as man and wife.

# Chapter Nineteen

Once Chris and Melian were joined in marriage, things moved very quickly. Several hovercrafts were ready to take off for Resurrection Ranch in Nevada.

The amount of personnel who were transferring there overwhelmed Mark. He understood the need for the hospital to be staffed by trained staff but the sheer numbers of people involved was staggering.

Another surprise came when Cassion and Hodia informed everyone that when the priest was at the complex they were wed in a private ceremony. When Mark asked why they hadn't had a more lavish affair, they told him without their families in attendance it was best if they were quietly mated.

"We aren't any less married," Cassion told him. "Had Melian wed someone from her own community, it wouldn't have been such an impressive ceremony. They would have presented themselves before the priest and said their vows privately. The Earthly ceremonies are definitely more complex."

Mark could understand what Cassion was telling him. He knew Kara had been excited about all the planning for Chris and Melian's wedding and it would be the same when the two of them were married.

~ * ~

At last, it was time for Mark and Kara to board the hovercraft that would take them to Nevada. Considering that, until Mark had been taken to Mexico, he could hardly remember ever being in a hovercraft, his first few flights awakened a flock of butterflies in his belly. The thought of flying above the earth had been frightening, but now it was exhilarating thinking about the future that lay ahead of them at the end of their flight.

As soon as the ranch came into view, Mark felt his stomach threaten to rebel. They headed toward the docking station. From the window to his right, he could see the main house. Other than that, the buildings he remembered were no longer there. It was evident his Uncle David had already begun clearing the way for the new construction.

They neared the docking station and the small dots he'd seen from the air turned into groups of people watching as each of the hovercrafts neared their destination. Even though he could make out groups, he couldn't distinguish one individual from another.

He could also see several trailers parked around the perimeter of the main area. They were sleek and modern. It was a certainty they would provide adequate shelter from the elements. Be it rain, cold or heat, the occupants would be comfortable.

As usual, the docking was flawless and without incident. The cabin depressurized and the doors opened. Hesitantly, Mark exited the craft first, in order to be able to help Kara as she stepped onto the land that had been his home for so much of his life.

"There's so much activity," she commented. "The house looks..."

"Don't say it looks nice. For me it's a house of horrors. While the Hendersons lived there in luxury, the only time we went there was to get our meals and our punishments. I hope something can be done to change its appearance."

"You must understand we are just beginning the rehabilitation of this property. Give it a few weeks and I'm certain all of the bad memories will be nothing more than a bad dream."

Mark prayed she was right. This ranch was meant to be a new beginning.

From across the yard, he saw a group of young men. He expected to be able to recognize the faces of the men he remembered when they were children. Instead, he was greeted by several strangers.

"Mark, is that you?"

He looked to the man who was approaching him, searching his memory. If it hadn't been for the man's voice he would have been confused as to his identity. Thankfully, he recognized the man as Clint

Anders.

Breaking into a wide grin, he hurried to clasp Clint's forearm. "I was shocked when Peter told me he'd found you, as well as Parker and Roger. I know we can work well together, like we did when we were kids."

"Speaking of Peter, where is he? You're the only one I've been able to identify other than the guys I was with on the ranch in Mexico."

"Peter is finalizing things back in Denver. He's met a girl by the name of Jerilyn, who will be coming here as a counselor. We've all talked with her and she's exceptional at what she does. Unlike the girl I plan to marry, she's an Earthling just like us. Chris just got married to a teacher from under the ice cap of Antarctica. My fiancée is also an alien, but she's from the dark side of the moon. We're planning to be married in the fall when her parents will be able to be here."

"I can't believe so much has happened in such a short period of time. When we got here, everything was pretty much like we left it. Then this guy named David Manning showed up and things have been progressing rapidly."

Mark smiled at the mention of his uncle. At the time they met, he'd been apprehensive, but the more they talked, the more David convinced Mark of his sincerity and dedication to the project that would mean so much to the former residents who would be coming to this ranch working toward a new life.

While Kara reunited with the medical personnel who accompanied them from Denver, Clint insisted on introducing the other men in his group.

Mark was still reeling from seeing his old friend. Even though he'd been rescued for several months, he still looked gaunt. He was beginning to wonder if any of the men suffered from medical issues caused by their enslavement.

"I know there are guys out there the authorities have yet to find, but this is Juaviar. He was with me on the ranch down in Mexico. He didn't come from here, but his parents were very poor and they actually sold him to support their other children. He's originally from Bolivia in

South America."

Mark clasped Juaviar's forearm. One by one the others were introduced. After meeting Juaviar, Parker, Roger, Ken, Jerry and Dennis, Mark decided it was best if he assess each of them as to their skills. He was also interested in their level of education as well as their needs.

As he made his way up to the house, he began to wonder if Diane, Buck and Terri had arrived. If they had, he certainly didn't want to intrude on their privacy.

Buck met him at the door, causing him to rethink his idea of interviewing the men at the main house.

"I'm glad you're finally here," Buck enthusiastically greeted him. "We got here a couple of weeks ago. Mom's been meeting with Uncle David and they've come up with some fantastic ideas. She's got coffee made and Terri baked some cookies. We know you can't work on an empty stomach, but we're excited to show you what we've already done to the house."

With trepidation, Mark followed Buck into the house. Visions of stepping across the threshold to enter the kitchen made him weak in the knees. He wished Kara was with him, but he knew she was busy consulting with the people with whom she'd be working.

Willing the weakness to go away, he closed his eyes for a moment, reliving the vision of the kitchen where Mrs. Henderson doled out the punishments that she deemed necessary to keep everyone in line. When he opened them again, he was surprised to see an ultra-modern kitchen that in no way resembled his memory of the house.

"Mark, it's good to see you again," Diane said. "Come in and sit down. I've got a snack ready for you. Uncle David should be here soon and together we can show you what we have in mind for this house. I know it's where we will be living, but it's way too large for the three of us. There's enough room for an office that is separate from the living quarters. I can hardly wait for you to see it."

Mark couldn't quite comprehend what Diane was talking about, but decided to wait until he saw what she was talking about before passing judgment.

Diane finished pouring the coffee and put a plate of cookies on the table, when David arrived.

"Has Diane showed you the office?" David asked.

"Not yet, we wanted to wait until you got here," Mark replied. "Diane thought I needed food before we took the tour. I think she had a good idea. I did need something to eat and these cookies look absolutely delicious. I don't remember eating anything but slop in this kitchen."

"I hope you're happy with what we've done with the remainder of this house. We wanted to erase all of those bad memories. This ranch is going to be a showpiece when we finally get everything done."

After eating, Mark felt much better. Terri and Buck led the way as they made their way throughout the first floor. Never having been further into the house than the kitchen, everything looked new and clean.

"Last but not least," Diane said, "here is your office."

Mark stared at the door that closed off the room where he would be conducting the business of the ranch. He held his breath as she opened the door. Inside, he saw a large, modern desk as well as a comfortable chair. Windows looked out onto the vast landscape that would soon be filled with facilities as well as cattle in the distance. There was even a door leading to the outside so he could come and go without bothering the family.

"We were looking forward to the future," Terri said.

Her statement took Mark by surprise. "What do you mean?"

"I know you are planning to be the ranch manager," she began, "but in time you and Buck will be running the veterinary clinic. Mom and I have been talking about what the future holds. I love the detail involved in managing a ranch. In time, I'd like to take over the job and free you up to do what you'll be trained to do. I'm also thinking about opening a dance studio. Sometime in the future maybe we can get youngsters from the age of two who are interested in learning to express themselves through dance."

Mark hadn't considered a woman ranch manager, but if Terri was sincere, he could see no problem with it. She was young enough to model her education to adapt to the needs of a ranch manager.

"I don't know what to say. I've been hoping one of the guys who will be working here might like the position, but if you're certain this is something that might interest you, I say why not?"

To his surprise, Terri threw her arms around his neck and kissed his cheek. "I was worried you'd think I was too young to make such a decision. I knew, the minute we arrived here, I wanted to be part of the operation. I discussed it with Mom and Buck and we all think I can handle it."

He suddenly felt something he'd never felt before. Family was such an alien idea to him. He hardly knew how to handle having siblings. The boys he'd shared the dormitory with were more like acquaintances. They certainly weren't family. With the exception of Peter and Chris, they were nothing more than kids he hardly knew. With all the hard work, there was no time for anything but sleep and work.

~ * ~

The next area he checked out was where the trailers were located. Each trailer had three bedrooms so they could easily accommodate at all of the men who came with Clint, leaving one trailer for Mark and Peter to share. He wished he could be sharing the trailer with Kara, but he knew it was impossible. She would be sharing with some of the other single women who came to help rebuild the ranch.

It came as a surprise, when he entered the trailer where he would be living during the summer construction period, to find his grandmother busy stocking the cupboards.

"I'm so excited to have you here," Anna said. "I've been in contact with your doctors and they told me what you should have in the line of snacks, so I've been busy loading your cupboards."

"It's not that I don't appreciate what you're doing, but I don't know how to cook."

"I didn't think you did. You haven't seen the dining hall yet. When we learned of the donation for the dining hall and kitchen, I made certain it was the first thing built here. It has a state-of-the-art kitchen and a young man has agreed to relocate here to be the chef. He's fantastic and he understands there will be a lot of hungry people here. He's excited about working here. We've been working out the logistics of everything we need. I think you'll be well satisfied. Until he can get here, Diane and I are doing the kitchen. When I told him one of the young boys wanted to learn how to cook, he was impressed as well as excited."

Mark was the first to admit that he hadn't thought of how meals would be served. In all of his life, he'd never had to think about something as mundane as food. It was always provided, no matter how terrible it was. It was now evident that meals, as well as other things he hadn't considered in the past, would be part of his job as ranch manager.

# Chapter Twenty

Mark was surprised at how quickly things progressed on the ranch. While the new hands successfully took over the care and feeding of the cattle, David and his crew worked on the various new structures being constructed.

He'd been on the ranch for a week when several new people arrived. The first to arrive were Peter and Jerilyn, followed a few days later by Chris and Melian. Mark couldn't believe how rested Chris looked. Even Melian seemed to glow. He wondered if she was already carrying Chris' child. It would be exciting to have new life on the ranch.

The next to arrive were Chris' Uncle George, Aunt Susan and their families. They were all staying at a hotel in the next town and seemed anxious to see all the work being done on the ranch that was owned by their tribe.

"I know I never saw this place when it was in the original condition, but I can see a future here for all of you," George declared. "What you don't know is that we were able to buy this ranch without a huge expenditure. With the Hendersons never being able to return, the state saw the potential for the future of this property and sold it to us for a dollar. It frees up a lot of cash for things you might need in the future. We've already invested in some prime breeding stock, both of cattle and horses."

"I don't know what to say. This is a lot more than I ever expected."

The expression on George's face said much more than any words. "I'm certain you don't know all of the history of our people. Horses have always been important to us. It has always been my dream to have a successful horse-breeding facility. This is a dream of mine and the elders have agreed this would be the perfect place for it to come true."

"I never thought about a breeding facility, but it makes sense.

There is certainly enough room here for not only the cattle but also the horses. Plus, I understand it's old-fashioned, but most of us have always worked with horses. I think it will be a great addition to the property."

"You think like a Cheyenne. Even though I know you have family of your own, I would like to become like another uncle to you."

George's suggestion warmed Mark's heart. He liked this man and would always be indebted to the members of his tribe for taking a chance on turning horrors into reality.

~ * ~

Mark made his way to the dining hall. It had been a long day and he looked forward to eating the evening meal. So far, everything Diane made was top notch. All the meals she served were completely healthy and fresh.

Across the room, Chris and Melian sat at a table for four with Kara. When Chris waved, Mark returned the gesture and headed over to sit with them.

"So," Mark began, "what do you think so far?"

"I'm in awe of everything that has been accomplished in such a short amount of time. We went over the plans for the educational facility with David this afternoon. Both Melian and I were duly impressed. Tomorrow we hope to start interviewing the men and decide what they're going to need for education."

Mark nodded his head. "I interviewed them as to their ranching abilities while you were on your honeymoon. I think you might have your hands full on the educational front. Many of them don't even know how to sign their own names At least we could recognize numbers and sign our names. I thought the Hendersons were unique in the way they treated us, now I'm beginning to wonder how many other facilities will be discovered in the months and years to come."

Within minutes, the food was served. As at the complex, the food was served buffet style. For working men, the meat was the main course. There were also vegetables, potatoes and salads to appeal to every person living and working on the ranch.

After filling his plate, Mark returned to the table. He could tell by the look on Kara's face she had something on her mind.

"I had a communication from my family," Kara said. "With all the interaction between the base on the moon and the bases here on Earth, the confederation has added four extra flights. Since my parents were scheduled for the fall flight, they were bumped up to come next month. Would you be upset if we moved the wedding up to coincide with their arrival?"

"Upset?" Mark questioned. "Why would I be upset? It's almost miraculous. I want the two of us to be together more than anything else in the world. Do you have any idea where we would hold the ceremony? We don't have a church on the ranch yet."

"We don't have a building, but a church can be anywhere. I actually would love to have an outdoor service and we could hold the reception here in the dining hall. Growing up on the dark side of the moon, being outside was never an option. Even at the complex in Denver, I didn't get outside as much as I would have liked. Here it is so refreshing to be outside, I think it would be the perfect setting for a wedding."

Mark was overjoyed at the change in their wedding plans. Originally, they were going to wait for a few more months and by that time a proper church would have been built. He'd seen the plans David drew up for the structure and agreed with them completely. Now, the idea of an outdoor wedding ceremony was more exciting than any building plans for the new church.

"I think that's an excellent idea. Hopefully, we can bring in another trailer for the two of us to use until our house can be completed."

"With as fast as the buildings are being constructed, it's entirely possible your house can be completed within the next few weeks," Chris observed. "Your Uncle David has been doing a fantastic job here."

~ * ~

Over the next month, Mark found himself immersed in not only the day-to-day running of the ranch and overseeing the building projects, but also into planning the wedding. He'd been so impressed with the Native American ceremony at Chris and Melian's wedding, he asked them if they would mind allowing those same ceremonies to be included in their wedding.

"Since Uncle George officially adopted you, I don't see why he would object. His tribe does own this land. That in itself is reason for the traditional ceremony to be performed. Why don't you communicate with him tonight and see if it can be arranged?"

"I was hoping that's what you'd say. I'm letting Kara plan most aspects of the ceremony, but this is something I want incorporated. I hope it will be as inspiring to her family as it was for me at your wedding."

That evening, Mark used his communicator to contact George Little Horse. As soon as he made contact, Mark knew he'd made the right move. George seemed to be overwhelmed with emotion when Mark broached the subject of having a traditional ceremony.

"I am honored, as I'm certain the shaman will be when I contact him. Keeping the old traditions alive is important to our people. In addition to your ceremony, I know the shaman would welcome the opportunity to bless the land as well as the rebuilding of Resurrection Ranch. I'll be looking forward to having you contact me with the final plans for your wedding."

"As soon as the plans are finalized, you will be the first person I call. You've already met my grandmother and Uncle David, but it will also give you a chance to meet Uncle Phil and Uncle Jon. For the first time my entire family will be together in one place."

As soon as the words left his mouth, he thought of his Aunt Cindy. It could be months or even years before she would be able to return to the states from Peru. At least all of the family he already knew would be there.

Mark closed the connection and smiled to himself. The traditional ceremony would be his contribution to the wedding, something that held meaning for him. He was certain Kara would agree. He remembered how impressed she'd been with the ceremony held at Chris and Melian's wedding.

~ * ~

"Are you certain this is something you should be doing?" Peter asked while they went over the day's assignments for the work day on the ranch.

"Of course, I am. Why would you ask such a thing?"

"You haven't known Kara for very long. Are you sure?"

"Are you sure of your feelings for Jerilyn?"

"You know I am, but she's not…"

"An alien? No, she's not. She was damaged by a guardian who abused her in ways we can't even fathom. If it weren't for the aliens, she wouldn't have been rescued. They're human just like us, only they have a different stature. I love Kara more than I ever thought possible. It's the same with Chris and Melian. You'll see, once you sort out your feelings, you'll understand why I'm anxious to make Kara my wife."

"I pray you're right. I want all of us to be happy. If being married to Kara makes you happy, then I wish you well."

# Chapter Twenty-one

Kara waited anxiously for her parents' shuttle to arrive at the ranch. She prayed they would approve of her marriage to Mark. Having grown up in her parents' strict household, she worried that they wouldn't be happy with her choice.

"Kara," her mother said as soon as she exited the hovercraft. "You look good. I am pleased to see how well life on Earth is treating you. I worried when you told us about your move to a ranch in the middle of nowhere. Now that I see how you're glowing with happiness, I can put my fears to rest."

"When do we get to meet your young man?" her father inquired after he gave her a loving hug.

"Soon, Father, very soon. For now, he's busy in his office, working on the management of the ranch. After that he usually checks out the progress being made on the apartment complex. It's almost complete, as it is where we will be living after the wedding."

"I thought you were having a house built," her mother said.

"We are, but for now there are other projects that need to be finished. The builders are working hard on the educational and medical facilities, as well as the bunk house for the men who are working with the cattle until everyone can be trained. They've also started work on the veterinary clinic and school. Hopefully, by this time next year, Mark and his brother, Buck will be able to begin their studies in veterinary medicine. Everything here is moving so quickly it's amazing."

"I remember when you first met him, you said that he had no educational skills whatsoever. How is it he can be ready for such advanced learning?"

Kara explained the accelerated education program both Mark and Chris participated in. "I wish you could have seen it for yourself. They were both like sponges, absorbing every bit of knowledge. By the time we left the complex, they were ready for secondary school classes. Those will start this fall, as several of the teachers from the complex have relocated here. You'll see, everyone is excited about this project."

"What about my brother, Gratan?" her mother inquired. "From his communications he's also relocated here. Is he happy? I mean, he certainly doesn't have a modern facility here like he did at the complex."

"When we moved here, Mark's uncle had a temporary office set up for him. Everyone has been working together to get the hospital completed. I think you'll be amazed when you see all the progress they've made. There are also several nurses from the complex who have come with us. We're all making our own contributions to this project."

Her parents agreed with her and together they made their way to the construction site for the hospital and clinic. She could tell they were impressed with the progress.

Things became even more comfortable when Gratan joined them. She knew Gratan missed his family, especially his sister, Kara's mother.

"I'll leave the three of you to get reacquainted. I have some things to take care of at my trailer. Mark and I will see you at the dining hall for the evening meal."

She crossed the dooryard and went to Mark's office at the main house. She found him sitting behind the desk working on schedules for the upcoming school year. The work on the ranch would still need to be done, but at the same time the men needed to obtain their educations.

"Are you at a stopping point?" she asked when she came into the office.

"For you, most certainly. Did your parents arrive safely?"

"They did. They'll be staying at Gratan's trailer while they're here. They asked me a lot of questions about your educational status. They said they found it hard to believe that you had accomplished so much in such a short period of time. I told them how hungry you were for knowledge and I think they were impressed."

"I'm done here for the day. It's almost time for the evening meal. I'll go back to my place and get cleaned up. I'll look forward to meeting your parents tonight at the dining hall."

~ * ~

Mark watched Kara leave his office. He'd tried to act as though he was comfortable with meeting her parents, but in reality, he was extremely nervous. He was thankful that his family was already at the ranch. While his grandmother, Uncle David, Diane, Buck and Terri had been with him since he first arrived from the complex, the remainder of the family arrived earlier in the week. His uncles Phil and Jon were there with Jon's wife Serena. It was good to have them there for moral support.

He was almost to his trailer, when he met Chris. "Hey Buddy, did your future in-laws arrive safely?"

"Kara said they did. She also said they seemed skeptical about how quickly we progressed with our educations."

"I don't blame them. There are times I can't believe how much we've learned in the past few months. I wanted to tell you Uncle George and several of the other members of the tribe arrived this afternoon as well. They contacted me after they checked in at the hotel. I don't know of anything else you could have done to make Uncle George happier. He brought Aunt Nancy, Aunt Susan and Uncle Robert along with him, as well as the shaman. This is going to be one special wedding."

"Like yours wasn't?"

"It was, but this will be the first wedding on Resurrection Ranch. It will show the hands that we are committed to making this a going operation."

"I think they already know that. I do worry about Peter, though."

"Why Peter?"

"We had a talk the other night and he thinks I'm jumping into marriage with Kara too quickly. Even though he has feelings for Jerilyn, I have a feeling he still mistrusts women. You remember how Henderson used to warn us not to have anything to do with them. He said it was because Kara is an alien, but I think there's more to it than that."

At the trailers, Mark and Chris parted company. They were both anxious to wash the dust and dirt of the day from their bodies, to prepare for the evening meal.

Once Mark finished in the shower, he donned a pair of dress pants with a button-down shirt. On any other evening, he would have dressed in clean jeans, boots and a t-shirt. For tonight he knew he needed to make a good impression on Kara's parents.

People were already arriving at the dining hall. He wished they had a private room, but one hadn't been built yet.

He was about to enter, when Terri intercepted him.

"Mom sent me to get you. She talked to Kara earlier and she and Grandma decided you shouldn't meet Kara's parents at the dining hall with so many other people around. The two of them prepared a meal for you. The rest of your family are coming for dessert."

Mark let out a sigh of relief. The more relaxed atmosphere of Diane's home would make this meeting easier.

As soon as he stepped through the back door, he could hear voices coming from the dining room. He steeled himself for the encounter with Kara's family. Before entering the dining room, he prayed Dr. Gratan would also be there. Considering the doctor and Kara's mother were siblings, he decided it might relieve the tension. It had been Dr. Gratan he consulted before asking Kara to marry him.

"We thought you'd never get here," Kara greeted him. "Mother and Father are anxious to meet you."

"As I am them. I needed to take a shower and change my clothes."

Kara's father was immediately on his feet. "There is nothing wrong with sweat of honest labor, my boy. Our daughter has told us many good things about you, as has my brother under the law. Gratan has the upmost regard for you. He told us that he gave his permission for your mating, since he was appointed as her legal guardian when we allowed her to go to Earth with him."

Mark glanced at Dr. Gratan. He was smiling, making Mark immediately relax.

"Dr. Gratan has saved my life more than once since I arrived at the complex. He is definitely more than just my doctor. I consider him to be my friend."

After the first interaction with Kara's parents, the evening became more relaxed than Mark originally thought it would be. He immediately liked the people who would soon consider him as part of their family.

The dinner Diane, Terri and Anna served rivaled anything Diane made for the men to eat at the dining hall. It was evident that she'd brought out some of her best recipes for tonight's dinner to make it special. They were getting ready to enjoy their dessert when David, Phil, Jon and Serena arrived to complete the family.

"What are your plans for the wedding?" Kara's mother asked.

Mark held his breath. How would these aliens take the fact he'd requested a Native American ceremony, in addition to the Christian one?

"Even though we don't have a priest from the moon here, the pastor from the church we attend in town has agreed to perform an outdoor service. After that, Chris' family, who are Native Americans, have agreed to perform a traditional ceremony. It's only fitting, because when this ranch was no longer in the possession of the Hendersons, their tribe purchased it and restocked it, with the provision Mark would return here to be the ranch manager. We witnessed the ceremony for our friends Chris and Melian. Mark wanted to incorporate it into our wedding festivities and I agreed. I feel like they are as much family as any of our blood relations."

"I have studied the history of Earth and in particular that of the United States," Kara's mother said. "The Native Americans have been of particular interest to me. I'm looking forward to your wedding day and seeing for myself what I've only read about. I have a feeling this will be one of the most interesting weddings I've ever attended."

# Chapter Twenty-two

Everyone on the ranch was excited to see the blessing of the ranch. Early on the morning before the wedding, George and the others from the reservation arrived just after dawn.

A blanket was spread on the ground with George, Nancy, Susan and Robert standing at each corner. They all wore ceremonial regalia and waited as the shaman who officiated at Chris and Melian's wedding came across the grassy area to begin the blessing.

"Tobacco and corn are used as sacrifices to the Great Spirit. We offer the sacred smoke to the North winds," the shaman said, as he handed the pipe to George who took a puff and blew the smoke toward the North.

The same process was repeated for each of the four directions, with each of the people standing at the edges of the blanket drawing the smoke from the pipe and blowing it into the wind.

"Last we offer sacrifices to the Mother Earth and Father Sky. Bless this ranch and those who will work here as well as those who come here to learn. Make it prosperous."

Mark could tell those who had not witnessed a Native American ceremony before were in awe of the pageantry and tradition that was as old as the world itself.

He turned to look at Kara's mother and was surprised to see tears in her eyes. Without shame, she wiped the tears that were rolling down her cheeks away with her hand.

"That was the most moving thing I've ever seen. I can hardly wait to see what the ceremony for your wedding will be like."

"This was impressive," Kara said. "Tomorrow will be even more so. I wanted to have it performed at my wedding when I saw it at Chris and Melian's wedding. I didn't know how to go about asking. When Mark told me that he'd asked Chris' family to do this for us, I was overjoyed."

~ * ~

Later that evening, the members of both Mark and Kara's family met at Diane's home for dinner. Along with them were Chris and Melian as well as his mother's side of the family.

"You realize you won't be able to see your bride after midnight tonight," Kara's father cautioned.

"So, I've been told," Mark replied. "It shouldn't be hard, since we both live in different trailers and usually don't see each other until the evening meal. I'm busy with the ranch as well as checking out the building projects and she's occupied at the clinic, such as it is. I'm certain once the hospital and clinic are finished, everyone who came with us from the complex to work in the medical facility will be happy to be out of their cramped quarters."

"I totally agree," Kara's mother said. "My brother gave me a tour of his offices today as well as a tour of the facility that is being built to house the hospital and clinic in the future. You must know you've been given an excellent opportunity here."

"I'm proud of everything that's happening here," Phil said. "My nephew and his friends have terrible memories of this place from growing up here. It is definitely a blessing, not only for Mark and Chris but for all of the young men they will be helping in the future. From what I'm told, the authorities are still finding survivors of this place."

Mark understood what his uncle was saying, yet he was far from healed of his anxiety. He still had nightmares about the days he spent living and working on this ranch. Those wounds, he knew, were psychological, while the scars he carried both within his body and on the outside were the product of the years he'd spent as a slave.

"Kara, as well as Gratan, has told us about your medical condition as well as the life you lived before you came to the complex," Kara's father said. "We will be proud to call you our son under the law. I worried about Kara coming to Earth. I was afraid she would never find a life mate here. It seems our concerns were unfounded."

Mark beamed at the compliment from Kara's family. Around the table, his family voiced the same opinion about Kara. He knew this was going to be a good union.

~ * ~

Although the wedding wasn't scheduled until afternoon, Mark found he couldn't sleep past six in the morning. Rather than trying to get back to sleep, he went down to the dining hall for an early breakfast before going over to the office.

Time seemed to get away from him, until at close to noon, Chris entered the office. "I thought I'd find you here," he said as soon as he stood in front of Mark's desk.

"I thought working would calm my nerves. This is a big step I'm taking. What if I don't know what to do on the wedding night?"

Chris chuckled. "Trust me, you'll know what to do. I'm certain Kara is having the same pre-wedding jitters. I know Melian and I did. We agreed to take things slow and everything worked out the way it should have."

"I'm sure they will," Mark agreed.

"In the meantime, your uncles, all three of them are looking for you. They finally came to me and asked me to help. I had a feeling I'd find you here. Now get your butt in gear. You have to get ready for your wedding."

Mark closed the computer he'd been working on and got to his feet. Chris was right. He had no business being in the office today. Of any day in his life, this was the most important one. In a matter of hours, he and Kara would be husband and wife.

~ * ~

Kara's mother, along with Melian, fussed over everything from her dress to the styling of her hair. Her mother brought along a wedding gown that looked like the ones the girls on Earth wore. The only difference was the purple trim that would intensify the violet of her eyes.

Melian was carefully styling Kara's platinum curls by weaving purple ribbons into a style that enhanced her beauty.

"Do you know what Mark is wearing?" Melian asked.

"He said his uncles on his mother's side of the family brought along a suit that depicted his Mexican heritage. I have a feeling he wasn't overly excited about it because of the treatment he endured while he was on the ranch in Mexico. In the end it doesn't matter. We are both honoring the heritage of our parents. Besides, when we participate in the Native American ceremony, we will be changing into the regalia George and Susan brought for us to wear."

"I will tell you one thing," Melian said, "once you wear the regalia, you'll be spoiled. Those were some of the most comfortable pieces of clothing I've ever worn. When it's just Chris and me, we often wear ours and just relax. I'm certain it will be the same with you and Mark."

Kara tended to agree. Yesterday Susan presented her with the dress she would be changing into for their special ceremony. It amazed her to feel how soft the doeskin dress was. She could only imagine it caressing her body.

~ * ~

In a repeat of the scenario that played out only months before at Chris and Melian's wedding, Mark waited for the ceremony to begin. The difference was that this time it was Chris who was working hard to calm Mark's nerves.

At last, the music denoted the beginning of the ceremony. While Mark and Chris took their places, they watched as Melian walked toward them. Her dress seemed to change colors with every step she took. At times it looked purple only to change to lavender as she came closer to where they waited for her.

As soon as Melian took her place beside the arch that had been erected in the place of an altar, all eyes turned to Kara as she and her father walked toward her future.

To Mark, Kara was even more beautiful today than he'd ever seen her look. The closer she came to him, the more he wondered how he had ever been so lucky as to have met and fallen in love with this woman who looked more like an angel than a flesh-and-blood human being.

With the religious ceremony completed, Mark and Kara returned to their respective trailers in order to dress in the regalia provided by George and Susan.

"I wish I could have worn these clothes for the wedding. I've never had anything so comfortable in my entire life."

Chris nodded. "I know what you mean. My family has been more than generous giving you these clothes. Melian and I wear them often when we want to relax. It will be the same with you and Kara."

By the time they returned to the area set apart for the wedding, the wedding arch had been replaced by the three piles of sticks. As soon as they approached the shaman, he lit the two outer piles on fire.

"The fire to North represents the life Mark lived before joining his life with Kara's. It is the same with the pile to the South. This is Kara's prior life. To seal your union, it is time for you to push your piles into the united one in the center."

As soon as each pile was pushed to the center, a cheer went up from everyone in attendance. Mark took it as a signal to take Kara in his arms and kiss her tenderly for the first time as husband and wife. He'd argued long and hard with the pastor, saying rather than share a kiss after the religious ceremony he wanted to wait until the second ritual was completed to claim Kara as his own.

"A toast to the bride and groom," Anna declared, once everyone was seated at the tables set up for the reception. "May they enjoy a long and happy marriage."

Her sentiments were echoed across the expanse of the lawn where everyone was gathered.

For Mark, the well wishes were the culmination of the journey he'd been making ever since he was a child of four years old, standing alone on the sidewalk outside of the apartment he shared with his mother. With Kara by his side, he would never be alone in this world again.

# About the Author

Sherry Derr-Wille began her writing career in her sophomore English class in high school. Challenged to get an A on the first test, she won the right to sit in the back of the room and write for a year. At the end of the year no one told her to stop the assignment, so she didn't. At her 40th class reunion, she realized she was the only one who enjoyed the assignment. It was too late because by that time she'd signed seventeen contracts for her work.

Wife to her high school sweetheart of over fifty years, she is the mother of three, grandmother of nine and great-grandmother of five. She is retired and lives in a mid-sized town close to the Illinois border in Southern Wisconsin. Her mantra is READ LOCAL AND BE TRANSPORTED TO ANOTHER WORLD.

### The Return of the Ancients
The Aliens Book One

Nina is devastated when she realizes she must leave Plantas along with the man who is to become her mate, Ragnar, and her best friend, Tarena. When Nina arrives on Earth in Peru at the Nazca plains, she is greeted by a young archaeology student, Rand Jacobson. Even though she is attracted to Rand, she is still grieving the loss of Ragnar.

Ragnar is surprised when, after being greeted as a god on the planet Seros, the military opens fire on his family. After being taken prisoner, he is treated like a lab rat until a scientist, Geni, comes to his rescue. At her estate, he learns the physicians who work with her have saved the lives of his family and friends.

### My Uncle the King
The Aliens Book Two

When three contingencies took off from their dying planet, Plantas, only two arrived at their destination unharmed. When the lost contingency is hit with a meteor storm, only one ship survives and makes it to their destination of Nalo. Over the generations, the descendants of the original refugees become the ruling class of their adopted planet. Even the rebel group, the Pure Of Nalo, are unable to unseat the monarchy. When relations with Earth are established, it is Prince Nicos who leaves Nalo to find love on an alien planet and bring back new ideas as well as his Earthly family to save the throne and the people of Nalo.

### You Again

While attending college at the University of Wisconsin in the 1960s, Carole Martinson fell in love and eloped with Phillip Vanderlin. When his parents realized she was a farmer's daughter and below them socially, they insisted they divorce.

Fast forward to 2019 and Carole is invited to a wedding cruise financed by her granddaughter's fiancé's grandfather. With no knowledge about the groom's family, Carole flies to Florida for the cruise she and her second husband never got to take. Upon her arrival, she immediately recognizes Phillip.

Phillip never forgot his first love. He is thrilled when he realizes the grandmother is the girl he was forced to leave behind so many years ago.

www.ingramcontent.com/pod-product-compliance
Lightning Source LLC
Chambersburg PA
CBHW070325130626
46556CB00007B/2729